WHEN THE STARS ALIGN

By

Wendy

Howard

When the Stars Align

Woodrow Publishing
www.woodrowpublishing.com/

ISBN:9798582400189

DEDICATIONS

This book is dedicated to

Stuart

Still going strong after all these years -
They said it wouldn't last but
We proved them wrong
X

CONTENTS

CHAPTER 1
ARRIVAL

As the plane began its descent, five minutes after the captain said it would, Laura looked out of the window. Far below she could see the blue ocean with tiny islands scattered here and there. As the plane became lower in its descent, the tiny sparkles dancing on the water turned into fishing boats bobbing up and down.

It had been a strange flight. Normally she would have been filled with anticipation about a new country to visit or a family reunion, but not today. Today she just wanted to get there as soon as possible and as far away as possible from the nightmare of the past few weeks.

She wasn't too keen on flying, she found it boring. And with no one to talk to, this flight had been even more boring than normal. Even though it was only a four-hour flight, it had seemed like an eternity. The seats seemed even more uncomfortable today, the meal was tasteless, and the cabin seemed full of screaming kids! She'd hated every minute of the flight, and her present bad mood was not about to change with what lay ahead before her.

She felt a strange sensation in her stomach as the plane continued to drop in height, at the same time her ears became bunged up and a little painful as the pressure took effect.

Gradually the little islands gave way to larger islands each with sandy coastlines. She could make out villages and fields and could see they were now over a large island. Maybe they were nearly there, but no, the plane headed out to sea again and towards another island.

Quite unexpectedly the plane turned sharply then levelled out. It seemed to be just skimming the waves below. Now it appeared to have almost stopped in the sky. Slowly it flew towards land. On her side of the plane she could see a mountain with hotels built in steps on its coastal side. They hovered over fields and deep valleys created by the once active volcanoes. After a few more seconds, the runway appeared. The plane bounced down upon the tarmac and hurtled along the runway, eventually slowing to what seemed a snail's pace and finally coming to rest outside the terminal building. She had arrived on the island of Kos.

From the beginning of May until the end of October the island's resorts were open to tourists from many countries, Germany, France, Italy, Poland, the United Kingdom and more, being dependent on the tourism season for its economic stability.

From the beginning of April you would see the owners of the tavernas giving a fresh lick of paint to the buildings, tables and chairs. Hotels began to clean their pools and tend to the gardens. Beaches were levelled by bulldozers after the winter storms, with sun beds and parasols sprouting up everywhere, being replaced for the coming season.

The traditional tourist shops filled their shelves with inflatables of every size, shape and colour. They restocked the bottles of suntan lotion and hung up the large beach towels and sunhats, ready hopefully for the coming invasion of sun worshippers.

Kefalos had always been one of the quieter resorts on the island favoured by couples, and many visitors came back year after year. The locals would make them feel special, remembering their names or what they liked to drink. So many people called this their second home, their little piece of paradise, and many first-time visitors fell under its spell and would return again and again, year after year.

Laura's mother and father, Jenny and John, had fallen in love with Kefalos on their first visit, and like many others they'd decided to make it their home. Sadly their plans were dashed when her father became terminally ill, but John had insisted that Jenny promised to continue with their Kefalos dream. So fulfilling this promise, she did.

After an amount of time living alone, Jenny eventually met and fell in love with a Greek man, Yiannis, even though after losing John she felt she would never love again. They were married and spent many happy years together. So Jenny found happiness here in Kefalos.

Laura wondered what the island had in store for her. Here, she was a single woman and fed up with her life, with her self-esteem in tatters and trying to get over a dreadful time in England.

'Well,' she said to herself. 'Here I am. Do your worst Kefalos!'

The usual jostling to get hand luggage from the overhead lockers ensued, followed by the customary wait until the steps were brought to the side of the plane and the doors were eventually opened. Moving along the aisle, slowly she arrived at the open exit where she caught her first glimpse of the outside and felt the wonderful warmth of the Greek daytime temperature. The sky was blue with not a cloud in the sky, so different to the grey skies and drizzle she'd left behind in Manchester, only a few hours ago.

If what her mum had told her was true, then this island was a truly healing place. She really needed it now. Strange as it seemed, even though her mother lived there for many years, Laura had only once visited Kos, and that was for her mother's wedding to Yiannis. Sadly that stay had only been for a couple of days because of her university commitments, so she'd seen very little of the island. She had planned to go and visit the next season but that wasn't to be.

Laura knew her mum and Yiannis would be here to meet her. She'd told them that as soon as she'd sold her flat she would be there for a visit, and now she was finally here. Even though Laura was now a grown woman, she really wanted, and needed her mum.

CHAPTER 2
LITTLE BOX OF MEMORIES

Selling the flat didn't take long at all. It was in an area close to the University and within easy travelling distance of Manchester and was in excellent condition, decorated in neutral colours with ultra-modern fixtures and fittings.

Laura had been quite surprised at the valuation, and stood to make a good profit on what she had originally paid for the property. To be honest, all she wanted was for it to sell as quickly as possible and get away. A few viewings had been arranged and the second couple who viewed it wanted it and were able to proceed quickly to completion.

Although she'd loved the flat and its location when she first moved in, she just could not live there anymore. She had acquired the flat with the money her dad, John had left her, and furnished it to her own designs. Luckily the buyers wanted most of the furniture and soft furnishings and had agreed a price for these also so she was leaving behind almost everything, except of course the basic essentials that she needed over the next couple of months, along with of course her treasured mementoes.

Now all that remained for her to do was pack the last cardboard box, ready for collection by the courier. This box would contain her treasures, things she'd collected over the years which meant a lot to her and brought back vivid memories from her past. She'd kept them packed in an old suitcase under the bed out of harm's way. Lifting the case carefully onto the bed, Laura looked inside at her box of treasure and thought that even though the items were individually wrapped, they would need more tissue and bubble wrap to ensure they were not broken during the journey.

She removed the first item, a snow globe which contained a scene of children playing in the snow. She shook it gently, and as she watched the snow fall it took her back to her childhood.

She'd been lucky to have had a happy childhood living up on the moors with Mum and Dad, along with her older brother and sister. Laura had always been the 'special gift' baby to her parents after the loss of Emily, the little one who'd been born prematurely and only lived for such a short time. She had many happy memories to look back on, but also had some heart wrenching memories too.

One of her earliest memories was of a magical Christmas when she was very young. Laura loved Christmas, but not just for the many presents she knew Santa would bring her, she really loved the run up to Christmas. She loved the way all the shops were so brightly decked out, the Christmas festivities at school and all the extra mail arriving each morning. She loved the annual visit to the loft to retrieve the decorations for the house and going with Dad to buy that year's Christmas trees. She revelled in the choosing of gifts for her family and friends and the constant sound of festive choirs singing songs everywhere they went.

She remembered the day when they drove into town to choose their Christmas trees, one for the lounge and one for the dining room. She knew it was still quite early when she threw back her duvet and shuffled over to the window. She pulled back the curtains and peeped outside, surprised to see that everywhere had been covered in a blanket of snow. It was everywhere, hanging from the branches of the trees in the orchard, lying on the roof of the stables and barn and the path that led to the back of the house. The surrounding fields and hills were covered too.

In the early morning semi-darkness the lights of the town far below twinkled like stars, making it a magical scene. She was sure Mummy and Daddy wouldn't mind if she woke them, they would just love to see this wonderful sight. She grabbed her dressing gown and battered old slippers and put them on, knowing that Santa would bring her new ones tomorrow because he always did.

She shuffled silently across the room and carefully opened the door trying unsuccessfully to avoid the loud creaking sound it always made as it swung open. She padded across the corridor to her parents' room and knocked softly on the door. She stood for a moment until a drowsy voice said, "Come in." She opened the door and could not control her excitement anymore. Running across the room she launched herself onto the bed, throwing her arms around her mother.

"It's snowing, it's snowing," she cried, her little face flushed and with her bright eyes shiny and alive with excitement. Her mother smiled.

Jenny knew how magical it was when snow fell, remembering her first Christmas in this house high on the hills when it had snowed on Christmas morning. Jenny and John had only been married a few months at that time and she had just found out that she was expecting her first child.

"Shall I wake Suzie and James?" Laura said with her voice full of excitement. "They must see."

Dad stirred and scratched his head, wondering what all the fuss was about.

"Come on sleepyhead," Laura cried. "Come and look through the window."

Her father sat up in bed and rubbed Laura's hair. He'd listened to his youngest daughter with his eyes shut tight pretending to be asleep. It had been difficult not to smile when he'd heard the excitement in her voice. He loved her so much and always looked upon her as a special gift. Laura had been their wonderful, much loved surprise.

A few years earlier they had lost a daughter, Emily, who had been born prematurely and only lived a matter of hours. It still hurt deeply when he thought about the loss, how he'd carried the tiny white coffin on the dreadful day of her funeral, and how for months he suffered such intense grief

14

that he was impossible to live with. His normal loving relationship with his wife, Jenny, had been stretched to the extreme limits.

Leaping out of bed he ran across to the window and threw back the curtains, feigning surprise at what he saw. Laura was delighted.

"I said you had to see didn't I? Isn't it great?" John had to agree. He loved the snow, especially when it was fresh and unspoilt as it was now. He loved living up here in the hills. The trouble with having an older brother and sister meant that they'd always done everything before and they seemed to know everything, so it was extra exciting to be able to show them something which they knew nothing about. She ran straight into Suzie's room, shook her gently to wake her and led her to the window to show her. Suzie smiled as she picked Laura up in her arms and held her at the window in silence watching the snowflakes swirling down and gradually adding more inches to the blanket.

On James's door in large black marker pen letters were the words - '**KEEP OUT** - that means you!' He'd been a bit grumpy of late. Mum said it was something called 'puberty.' Laura had wondered if it was catching, because she didn't want to be grumpy like her brother, James.

She hesitated but then knocked loudly on the door. "Go away," was shouted in a grumpy voice.

"Ha Ha" shouted Laura in a sing song voice. "You don't know what we all know."

"Don't care!"

"OK Grumpy. You'll be sorry you missed it."

A few minutes later, James staggered out of his bedroom still half asleep, his mop of dark hair sticking out at all angles and his hand covering his eyes to protect them from the glare of the landing light. Without speaking to anyone he made a beeline for the bathroom. When he re-emerged his hair was neatly combed and his eyes were alert. He smiled at Laura, who had remained waiting outside his bedroom door.

15

"Okay," James requested. "Show me what all the fuss is about, and why you have woken me up at this ungodly hour!"

Laura took his hand and led him to the landing window. Like his father had done before, James feigned surprise for Laura's benefit. She could be a bit of a pain, but he loved her just the same.

Little Laura couldn't wait to get outside and quickly pulled on trousers and a jumper. Her wax jacket and boots were in the usual place next to the back door. Owning horses meant that this was standard attire most mornings when feeding and mucking out was required. She ran down the path leaving small boot prints in the freshly fallen snow. Twirling round and round she held her face up to the sky as the snowflakes fell on her bare nose and cheeks, giving them a warm, rosy glow. She bent down and made snowballs, throwing them willy-nilly about the garden.

"Let's make a snowman" she called to the rest of the family, who still hadn't ventured outdoors.

"Breakfast first," Mum called.

"But it might be gone by then," cried a disappointed Laura. She gathered a handful of snow, put it in her pocket and then went inside for breakfast.

After she had eaten, she went back to her coat and put her hand in the pocket to find the lining was wet through but no snow remained. She was so upset until her dad explained that snow was only frozen water and could not be kept in your pocket.

John returned from work that night with an early Christmas present for her, a beautiful snow globe. "Now you can always have snow," he'd told her.

This snow globe was one item she'd kept and cherished over the years, even taking it to her student accommodation when she went to university. She now wrapped it extra carefully and placed it inside the large cardboard box.

The next item she took out from the case was a small velvet covered box. She opened it and inside was a variety of medals mounted on brightly coloured ribbons. She picked one out of the box, a riding club medal which made Laura smile.

Suzie, her sister, had always been involved with the horses. Each weekend her parents took her to various shows where she competed. Laura sometimes went with them and at one time she'd won a medal for completing a clear round in the novice ring, but that was her only involvement in horse riding.

Laura was the sibling who liked to dance. Even as a small child she had reacted to music in her baby bouncer. Her mother had talked about ballet lessons, but Laura said she didn't want to do that sort of dancing. One day she was watching the television and suddenly jumped up and down.

"That's it" That's the dance I want to do, like those girls with the pompoms," Laura announced. It was the new craze of dancing, a combination of the cheerleading routines predominantly favoured in America but without the gymnastics, a choreographed dance performed to music.

Her mother had found a local group that had an infant section. Laura was taken there and immediately learned the routines. She quickly became proficient as a lone dancer or as part of the team, and she loved it. They trained one evening a week and weekends if they weren't at competitions. She won her first ever medal at the famous Blackpool Tower competition. You could catch her in her bedroom in front of the mirror practising her moves, along with the fixed smile that went with it.

She'd definitely caught the bug. So from the age of five until her teenage years she competed all over the country, winning various medals and trophies. She loved it and it kept her fit. She always got a dancing part in school performances and it added to her confidence. Laura even considered taking a college course in performing arts but changed her mind for a more academic course, which she thought would be a better career choice for the future.

17

She placed the medals back in their box and placed it in the large cardboard box. Again she took out another item from the case, this time it was a police badge. Although it was probably from a local fancy dress shop, at the time Laura had thought it was real.

Even though she was not really keen on the idea, her mother had allowed her to have a Facebook account. Mum checked it regularly and could see she had several friends from school on her profile and most conversations were about homework, which teachers they liked or disliked, and what boy bands they thought were the best.

Laura had been a member of Facebook for some time when she got a new friend request. Mum had told her to always let her see who it was before she replied but he was the same age as she was, so she felt it should be okay to accept.

Today, Mum was out shopping and Dad was seeing to the horses. Laura looked at the photo. It was that of a young boy named Carl, who looked about the same age as her. When she accepted the request, she was able to look at his profile. He went to a school out of town, was an only child and he liked music.

Almost immediately he sent her a message saying thanks for accepting his friend request. He hoped they could become true friends and asked about her family. He said she was lucky to have a brother and a sister as he did not. His dad had left them and he was often left on his own because his mother worked. Laura felt sorry for him. They chatted regularly, telling each other what they were up to and Laura looked forward to their chats.

One day out of the blue he suggested that she should come over to his house, as his mum had left him on his own and he felt lonely. Laura went to ask Mum if she could go to see him.

"Who is he?" he mother asked. Laura told her about the friend request he'd sent, which she'd accepted but had forgotten to tell her mother about it. "Show me, Laura," her mother demanded, not looking at all pleased.

They went together and sat at the laptop in Laura's room and logged into Facebook. Sure enough, Carl was live. Jenny studied the young lads profile but thought it looked a little suspicious, maybe fake. She was about to block him when he sent a message to Laura.

'Are you coming to see me? I am very sad and alone. You are such a nice person I know you would make me feel better. We could hold hands and be real close' - Jenny winced when reading this last line.

"Okay, tell him you can't come today but maybe one day soon," her mum suggested. Laura typed the message.

'Okay, but I really wanted to be with you and hug you today. You are so beautiful,' Carl returned, making Jenny feel even more uneasy.

"Tell him you will message him tomorrow," she demanded. They logged off Facebook and mum tried to explain to Laura that she didn't think this person was nice at all.

"But he's the same age as I me and he's lonely. And Mum, he always says nice things to me," Laura pleaded.

Mum told Laura not to go back on Facebook until she had her permission. Jenny thought it best to get in touch with the authorities concerning her suspicions, so spoke to the local police. They put her in touch with one of the special officers who told Jenny they would come round to see them.

A young woman arrived a little later and asked Laura to log on to Facebook and show her Carls profile. The officer, named Petra, scrolled down the pages and looked at the conversations and messages which they'd sent to each other. It did appear at first glance to be a perfectly innocent conversation, but as Petra knew, paedophiles were very accomplished at making friends with young children by being kind and complimentary to them.

"Laura, I am going to try and explain to you why I don't think Carl is who he says he is," the officer began.

"But he's my friend," Laura pleaded.

"I understand that, but there are naughty men who pretend to be young boys so you will be friends with them," Petra explained.

"But why would they do that?" Laura questioned with innocence. Mum shook her head at the officer. She didn't want to say too much of which Laura was too young to comprehend.

"Do you think you would like to help me so we can find out if this is a bad man pretending to be Carl?" Petra questioned. Laura looked confused so the officer explained more. "I am going to ask you to message Carl, but type exactly what I tell you, okay?"

"Okay" confirmed Laura, still not understanding what was happening.

"Hi Carl, are you feeling better today?" Petra said. The message was sent.

He replied, 'A bit, but I'm still feeling lonely."

"Maybe I could come over to cheer you up," the officer dictated and Laura typed.

'That would be great,' Carl replied.

"Where can we meet?" Petra typed.

'Near the park entrance in town,' was the reply.

They made arrangements about the meeting time, but then he sent a further message which sent a chill down the officer's spine!

'Why don't you wear that nice short dress you had on in the photograph with you and your friend, the one you put on Facebook? You look very beautiful in that picture.'

"Okay I will, and I'll ring you when I get there," the officer dictated.

20

Having typed everything just as she was asked, Laura felt quite important to be helping the police. Petra made a few telephone calls and then they had a chat with Laura's mother. Jenny was a little worried that they were using Laura as bait, but if it saved other girls from being led on in this way it needed to be done.

Laura caught the bus as arranged. Mum couldn't go as Laura had put pictures of her and Dad on Facebook, so she might be recognised. The nice lady officer sat behind Laura on the bus, but didn't speak to her.

They'd arranged that Laura would ring Carl when she left the bus to tell him she was on her way and ask him if they were going to his house or staying in town. When she phoned, it was the voice of an older person who answered the phone. He said he was Carl's father, however on Facebook, Carl had told Laura that he did not have a father. The man said that 'his son' Carl had asked him to pick Laura up and take her back to his house, as he didn't have the bus fare to get into town.

Luckily, Laura's phone was being monitored, with everything being recorded. When she finished talking on the phone she received a message from the police incident room saying to go and meet the man, "But say you cannot go with him."

Laura walked to the park entrance. A man was standing just to one side of the gate. She was being very brave. The man moved forward.

"Are you Laura?" he questioned.

"Yes," she replied.

"I am Carl's dad," the man informed her. A lady pushing a pram sat on the wall next to the park entrance.

"I thought I was meeting Carl here," Laura told the man. "I'm sorry, but I cannot come anywhere with you. My mum wouldn't like it." Hearing this, the man suddenly grabbed hold of Laura's arm.

"You WILL come with me!" he demanded angrily. "I want to see more of you. You have a lovely little body!"

Laura wanted to scream. He took her arm and began to drag her towards the park entrance. The woman with the baby in the pram looked up.

"She's being a naughty girl," the man said. "She's trying to run away from me."

He gave another tug on Laura's arm. As he did this, the lady suddenly stood up and walked towards them. At the same moment a man appeared from behind the stone column of the park entrance.

"Police!" he shouted, to the shock of the perpetrator.

It all happened quickly. They arrested the man and he was escorted into a waiting police car. Officer Petra ran to Laura and hugged her.

"Good girl, you were so brave," Petra told the youngster. "Come on, let's go and get an ice cream, but after I phone your mum." Jenny was extremely relieved to receive the call, but also very proud of Laura.

It was later revealed that this man pretending to be ten year old 'Carl' was part of a well-known paedophile ring, and Laura had had a lucky escape. The lady police officer, who was now her friend, Petra, came to see Laura and gave her the police badge.

"Laura, you are now a special member of the police force," Petra smiled whilst giving Laura the badge which was now a prized possession, even though it reminded her of a not so happy memory!

Laura put the badge back into the box. She shivered when thinking about what might have happened had she not told her mum.

The next item in the case was an identity bracelet. One side was engraved with her name and on the other, Chris.

This had been a gift from a boyfriend Laura had been dating for a few months whilst at high school. They'd met through a school friend who introduced them to each other at a house party. Both were a bit shy and awkward when they first spoke, but by the end of the evening they were getting on quite well.

Chris offered to walk Laura home, but she explained that she lived on the Moors and was being picked up by her father. They said their 'goodbyes' and that was that - it seemed. However, a few weeks later, the friend who'd held the party was speaking to Laura.

"How did you get on with Chris?" she asked.

"Okay," Laura replied.

"Have you seen him since?"

"No."

"He seemed quite keen on you when I spoke to him."

"Really?"

"Don't you want to see him again?"

"Not bothered either way," Laura replied somewhat nonchalantly.

"Okay, I'll get him to meet up with you. How about at youth club on Friday?" the friend suggested.

"Okay," Laura confirmed.

When Friday came, Laura wasn't sure if she really wanted to go. It had been good chatting that evening at the party, but did she really want to see him again? She wasn't sure. She did like to go to the youth club though as they played good music there and she liked to dance, so she decided she would make an effort and go. She knew lots of people there, mates from school and friends of friends and soon found herself a group of people to talk and hang around with.

Chris arrived and sauntered over to join them. They chatted for a while and then he asked if she wanted to dance. They danced without speaking until the music slowed. Chris held up his arms to her to ask her to dance directly with him. Laura slipped into his arms and rested her head on his chest. They slow danced for a while and when the music finally stopped, they walked back to the seats and talked. Finally the time came for the youth club to close. Because she lived out of town, again her father was picking her up. This time Chris left nothing to chance.

"Can I have your phone number so we can arrange to go out together again?" he asked. Laura was happy to give it to him as once again, she'd enjoyed his company and wanted to see him again.

That was the start of the relationship. Laura agreed to see him at weekends as she was deep into her studies, wanting to get good grades in her exams so she could go to University.

They did crazy things together and had fun at the weekends. They travelled around the country to music gigs, climbed mountains and visited many places of interest.

Chris was besotted with Laura and would do anything for her. However, he became a little bit like a lapdog, always trying too hard to please her. Although she liked Chris, she found him a little boring and predictable. His first fumbled attempts at being intimate didn't arouse any feeling in her. He made a good friend, kind and caring, but she could never accept him as a lover.

When the time came for her to go to university, it was a welcome excuse for Laura to stop seeing him. He seemed quite devastated that their relationship shouldn't continue.

"We can write and see each other at half term," he said.

"Okay, let's see how it goes," Laura replied. She didn't want to upset Chris because he was a really nice guy.

When she was leaving for University he showed up to say goodbye and give her a gift, handing her a little box. When she opened it, it was a silver identity bracelet with both their names engraved on it.

"So we are always together," he told her.

"It's beautiful," she told him. "Thank you so much."

She wore it a couple of times over the next few days, but then she returned it to the presentation box and placed it in her memories box. It reminded her of the fun times they'd had together.

Laura sighed as she packed it away in the cardboard box. Another part of her life remembered.

Next she carefully unpicked at layers of tissue wrapping paper which held a pressed flower. She heaved a deep sigh of relief when finding it still intact. This was the rose that had been given to her at her dad's funeral.

It had been an awful time for Laura, seeing her normally fit and healthy father becoming a shadow of his former self. It had been a rollercoaster ride during his illness. On good days they walked in the hills, laughing and joking about what life had given them. On bad days when mum would sit with him, the three children comforted each other not knowing how long it would be before Dad left them forever.

Laura clearly remembered the night they went to say their last farewells. Dad told her he was proud of her. He said that when he was gone from this life, he would always be close.

"Look to the stars and that's where I will be, watching over you. I will be with you always," he told her.

The funeral had been heart-breaking. She was just a young girl really. She'd stayed with her grandparents the night before and travelled in the car with them. When they arrived at the crematorium, everyone spoke in whispers. Four pallbearers lifted the coffin from the hearse and began to carry it inside. This was the first funeral that Laura had ever attended and she really wasn't sure what to expect. She took a deep breath to try to compose herself. The coffin had been placed on the podium at the front, behind the opened curtains.

The vicar greeted all the family and ushered them to their seats. James sat on one side of his mother and Suzie on the other, whilst Laura sat next to James. Quiet music was piped through the chapel and the family held hands. They all knew how difficult it was for each other. Hymns were played but many people could not sing, being far too upset, emotional and choked up. James stood and read the lesson.

"What has a man if he has not love?" James began, but stumbled, overcome with emotion. When he finished, he took his seat back down beside his mother and gave her hand a squeeze.

Suzie was next and she read a poem that she'd personally written, telling of her love for her father and his love for her.

Next it was her mother, Jenny. Although her legs were like jelly she walked proudly to the lectern, holding it tightly for extra strength as she began the address.

But then came the moment that all of them had been dreading, the actual committal when the curtains closed and she could no longer see the coffin. Sad music began to play as the coffin was lowered out of sight and the red velvet curtains could be seen and heard, as they slowly began to pull together.

Laura could not control herself any longer. She called out "DADDY" and burst into hysterical sobbing. Suzie and James wept silently, but her mother stood tall and straight.

"Goodbye John," her mother, Jenny whispered. "Goodbye darling."

Each of the family was given a rose to remember him by. Laura kept hers safely inside her box of treasures. With a tear in her eyes, she wrapped it securely again and placed it inside the box for collection. Oh how she missed her dad. The hurt never went away.

Into the box she delved again and pulled out her university prospectus. It seemed so long ago, when she'd been so full of hope and ambition. She'd thrown herself into her studies after the death of her father, wanting to become the person he'd said she could be. When her exam results came back as excellent, she was offered places at several universities. She decided to go to Manchester, and this was here where she met Martin.

Laura joined all the usual student groups, the debating society, the theatre group, and even volunteered for various charity events. She filled every minute with study and activities.

During one lecture she found herself sitting next to a dark-haired attractive boy. He contributed eloquently to the question and answer sessions and Laura found herself mesmerized by his animated speaking. He suddenly turned towards her and she was caught looking directly at him. She smiled in embarrassment at having been caught out, but he just returned her smile with a smile of his own.'

"I'm Martin," he said gently. "And you are?"

"I'm Laura," she returned.

That had been the start of their relationship. They studied together and had fun together. They even graduated together. In the box she found a picture of her graduation, complete with her gown and mortarboard. She smiled when she remembered the occasion. Graduation had been a turning point in her life.

"Hi, it's Laura," she said on the phone to her mum. "How are you? I have loads to tell you and something to ask you."

'Me too,' thought her mum, but she wanted to tell the entire family together and certainly not over the phone.

"I've passed my exams with honours," Laura revealed. "What do you think of that?"

"I'm thrilled for you darling, you clever thing. Who would have thought it? You must have got your brains from me," Jenny laughed. "When did you find out?"

"They phoned me from uni last night," Laura explained. "I got the highest marks for the whole of my year."

"Excellent sweetheart," the proud mum gushed. "I am so pleased for you, and your dad would have been so proud too."

"I get presented with a special award at the graduation ceremony and that's what I am phoning to ask about. Do you think you could come over to be at the ceremony? Its two weeks' from now. I know its short notice, but the rest of the family are coming and I would love it if you could make it too," Laura requested.

"I'm sure I will be able to make it. I wouldn't want to miss it for the world," Jenny stated.

"Great," Laura said. "Sort a flight out and let me know the details so I can pick you up from the airport."

"Do you mind if I bring someone with me?" her mum said after a short pause.

"No problem. I can invite who I want to the presentation and thought we would arrange a family meal afterwards, what do you think?"

"That sounds great, love. I will let you know the flight details as soon as possible, once I've spoken to the airline."

"OK Mum," Laura said. "Incidentally, who are you bringing?" she queried.

"Wait and see," Jenny replied mysteriously. "Bye Honey."

"But... But... Okay, bye mum," Laura conceded.

A couple of weeks later, Laura waited at the arrivals section of the airport, clinging to the rope which cordoned off the area directly in front of the door through which arriving passengers slowly filtered out.

She fixed her gaze on the door and waited expectantly as tired travellers hauled heavy cases through, searching the awaiting crowd for waiting relatives. As soon as her mum came through, Laura pushed forward to greet her with tears streaming down her cheeks. They hugged for ages without saying a word.

"The car's just on the next level. Where's your luggage?" Laura said, breaking the embrace and the silence.

Mum suddenly turned round as if she'd forgotten something. Laura looked in the direction of her mother's gaze and saw a dark-haired man struggling through the double doors with a trolley piled high with cases and boxes. The man smiled at her mother.

"Laura I have someone I want you to meet," Jenny revealed. "This is Yiannis, and Yiannis, this is my youngest daughter, Laura." Yiannis extended his hand towards Laura and smiled, his eyes lit up as Laura smiled back.

"Pleased to meet you," she said shaking his hand and then kissing him on the cheek. "We guessed it must be a man who Mum was bringing because of all the secrecy" She noticed her mother's cheeks turning red. "Have we met before," asked Laura. "I feel like I know you." Yiannis shrugged his shoulders.

"I think not, but maybe," he replied.

Laura released the boot of the car and then opened the door for Jenny to get in. "What a dish," she whispered to her mum as she slid into the car. "Are there any more like him at home?" Laura laughed. Jenny winked at Laura but said nothing.

Forty-five minutes later they were nearing the village where Laura now had her flat. As they pulled into the car park in front of the apartment block, a first-floor window was flung open and a hand was frantically waving at the car. It was Suzie.

"My other daughter," Jenny told Yiannis, as she waved just as frantically back towards the window.

They unloaded the car and Yiannis carried the heavy cases, whilst Jenny and Laura balanced the boxes between them. The door of the flat was flung open and Suzie emerged with a broad smile on her face. She tried to hug Jenny despite the boxes. Yiannis stood behind her, smiling as he witnessed the love and joy this family were sharing.

Before Jenny could introduce Yiannis to Suzie, Laura shouted, "Just look at what mum brought with her," she laughed pointing appreciatively towards Yiannis, who stepped forward to meet Jenny's elder daughter as she looked him up and down.

"You win, Laura," Suzie smiled. "He has dark hair" Yiannis frowned, confused. "We were taking bets about what you would look like," Suzie explained. "I said fair and Laura said Dark. I'm very pleased to meet you."

"I am Yiannis, I'm pleased to meet you too," the good looking Greek man replied. He then made the observation, "You look just like your mother."

"Oh God do I" Suzie laughed.

"Can we get inside please so that I can put these parcels down?" pleaded a now impatient Jenny.

It was the first time she'd seen Laura's flat and was impressed by what she saw. It was very tidy, tastefully decorated and nicely furnished.

"Sit down and make yourselves at home," Jenny and Yiannis were told. They both sat on the pale grey leather sofa and they soon started to relax.

"There are some gifts in the boxes," Jenny said, knowing how Laura was always impatient as a child to open presents. "Is Jamie coming?" she then asked.

"Yes, he'll be here soon, but said he won't be able to stay long because he's on call tonight." Just as Laura said this, the door opened and they were all surprised to see Jamie and his wife, Caitlin entering.

"Managed to get away early. All quiet on the western front," Jamie joked. "Hi mum, give us a hug." Jenny stood and embraced her son. He was now so tall and handsome, just like his father had been at that age.

"Jamie, I'd like you to meet Yiannis" Jenny announced. Yiannis stood and everyone could see that he and Jamie were both about the same height. Jamie shook Yiannis firmly by the hand.

"I see Laura won the bet," Jamie laughed. "Have we met before? Perhaps when I was in Kos? You do seem very familiar."

30

"It seems everyone knows me" Yiannis smiled.

"So, you are from Kefalos?" asked Jamie.

"Yes, I have lived there all my life" Yiannis replied.

"And what do you do?" Yiannis told him. "Any children?" Jamie interrogated.

"Sadly no," was Yiannis' answer.

"Jamie!" Jenny shouted, coming to her Greek boyfriend's rescue. "You sound like the Spanish Inquisition!"

"Just like to know who's messing around with my mum," Jamie observed. Jokingly, Jenny hoped.

"Messing around," said Yiannis, looking worried. "I don't understand - messing around." Jenny spoke to Yiannis in Greek.

"Hey come on mum, English please," Jamie argued. "We want to know what you are telling this guy about us reprobates."

Yiannis turned to look at the expectant faces before him. "I do not mess with your mother. I love her!" he revealed, to which a deathly hush filled the room.

It was Jamie who spoke first. "And just what are your intentions regarding our mum?" he asked, somewhat aggressively Jenny thought.

"My intention is to marry her," Yiannis said. "That is if I have your permission?"

There was a pregnant pause before Jamie spoke. "Well that's okay then," he observed and everybody laughed.

Jenny thought back to how she'd practiced endless speeches broaching the subject of her marriage to Yiannis and all the counter arguments, if any problems had arisen. Happily it now seemed, they had all been unnecessary. She looked across at Yiannis, who was now happily chatting with Jamie and his wife. He seemed totally at ease with her family and she smiled to herself, knowing it was all going to be okay. She knew, and now her family knew that Yiannis was the right man for her.

The graduation ceremony went ahead the next evening. When Laura walked on the stage to receive her special award, Jenny couldn't have been any prouder. She glanced at Yiannis who was clapping enthusiastically. He had tears in his eyes and he looked so proud, as if it were his own daughter collecting the prize. He turned and smiled at Jenny and she gulped back the tears. What a lovely and caring man he was.

After the ceremony they piled into the cars and drove the short distance to the restaurant, where Laura had arranged the meal. Once they had eaten, Jamie stood up and everyone turned to face him.

"I know this is a very special night for Laura, and we all know how proud Dad would have been if he were here with us today. He would have been standing here now rather than me, proposing a toast to his youngest offspring. So in his place, as the man of the household it falls on me to say a few words.

Congratulations Laura. We are all thrilled with your achievements. Who would have thought that the baby would turn out to be such a genius? Well done. We love you." With this said they all stood, raised their glasses and toasted Laura.

"Now before I sit down," Jamie continued, "I have a few more things I would like to say. I think I speak for the rest of us when I say that when dad died we were all devastated, but mum especially. We were all worried when she insisted on still moving to Kos as she and dad had planned, and did not understand why. This was until we visited her and saw the island and met the wonderful people she knew there.

We could see that being there was healing her in a way we couldn't begin to understand; yet we knew she was still lonely. She and dad had been together so long it must have been so difficult for her to be on her own.

We hoped that one day she might meet someone special, but we knew it would have to be someone extra special to take Dad's place and mend Mum's heart," Jamie turned to face his mum's new man and said, "And enter, Yiannis." This received a rapturous round of applause, as Jenny's only son continued.

"Dad would be pleased that you have found someone to share your life with, Mum, and we are pleased for you also. Go for it, Mum. You have all our blessings."

"To Mum and Yiannis," everyone echoed, standing and raising their glasses again.

"Thank you," was all that Jenny could manage to say before tears choked her. She looked around the room at all the family, knowing she loved them all so dearly and felt so much love in return. She also knew how difficult it must be for all of them to accept a replacement for their father.

Yiannis stood. "May I say a few words," he said, hesitating when everybody clapped in encouragement. "May I begin by offering my congratulations to Laura on her wonderful achievement, and thank you Laura for letting me be part of the celebration," He raised his glass towards Laura.

"Thank you, Yiannis," Laura returned, accepting the congratulations offered.

"I would like to tell you a bit about myself and how I met your mother," Yiannis continued. "My story is similar to Jenny's. Like her, I was married to a very special person who I loved so very much, but she sadly died and I felt my life had ended that day. Unlike your mother I had no children, much as we'd wished to have them. So, you see I was very alone.

One day I was visiting a little beach, which had been a special place where my wife and I had often visited, when I had a little accident. I fell into the sea and knocked myself out on the rocks and would have drowned if your mother had not rescued me." All the family turned to look at Jenny in astonishment. She'd never told any of them about this.

"Mum?" Laura questioned, but received a blank expression from Jenny in return.

"She came to see me at the hospital. Instantly I felt like I knew her, but then she ran off," Yiannis remembered, continuing with the story. "I searched for her for ages and eventually found her. When we chatted, I found out that she too had tragically lost someone she loved and we were able to give comfort to each other.

Over the past few months we got to know each other far better and she told me all about you, her family, and how much she loves you all. I began to realize I was falling in love with your mother and that is why I have asked her to marry me.

Since then I have been worried about what you would all think, because I could tell from the way Jenny spoke about you that you all loved your father very much and I wondered if there was room for me in your lives." Admiring glances from the family were received as he said this, which gave Yiannis the confidence to continue.

"I just want to say I love your mother with all my heart. I want her to be happy and I would never do anything to harm her or any of you. She was really worried about telling you all about me, but can I just say, I love her so much...." He couldn't continue any longer as he was overcome with emotion. As he sat down, there was not a dry eye in the room.

A few months later it was the week of the wedding. Unfortunately, because of work commitments most of the family could only take a few days off, Laura being one of them. This meant she was unable to see much of the island.

The wedding took place on the little island in Kamari Bay, a popular place for weddings, especially with tourists who'd fallen in love with Kefalos and wanted to get married there.

Laura placed the university prospectus back inside the packing box and returned to the case. There was a document here, a little crumpled, but you could still read it. It was the transcript of a tarot card reading.

"How do you fancy going to have your cards read?" asked her friend, Viv. "It'll be fun."

"I'm not sure," Laura said. "I don't really believe in it."

"It doesn't matter if you believe or not," Viv instructed.

"She might tell me something terrible is going to happen, and then I'd be worried all the time," Laura admitted.

"Don't be such a softy," Viv laughed. "I'll phone and make us an appointment for tomorrow night, if she can fit us in."

"Okay, if you really want to," Laura finally agreed.

Viv called the name on the card she'd been given and when the lady answered, she confirmed the next evening was free and she could start them both from eight o'clock.

"I wonder if she's a bit spooky!" they said laughing.

"She might live in a weird house, with mirrors and candles everywhere!" Laura laughed, but she was still a little nervous about going

They found the house. It was a lovely old cottage with leaded windows and window boxes. As they announced their arrival by ringing the doorbell, a young woman opened the door.

"Come in," she said cheerily. 'Not a bit spooky looking' Laura thought. "I'm Frances," the young, pleasant looking lady said.

She took them into a large lounge, furnished with comfy chairs and muted lighting. "Please come in and get comfortable," she invited the two visitors.

Laura surveyed the room. It was traditional decor in keeping with the age of the house. A little table was in front of a cushioned chair. Placed upon the table was a pack of cards. Frances settled herself in readiness.

"Now before we start, can I get either of you a drink?" the tarot reader questioned politely, but both girls declined the offer.

"Have you ever had the cards read for you before?" Frances asked. They both said no. "Let me tell you a little about Tarot then." Frances then went on to explain about the origins if the cards and how they were read, the various meanings of each card and that sort of thing.

"Do you have any questions?" Frances eventually asked the pair, to which they both shook their heads. "Okay then, who's going first?" Viv said she would go first, so Frances asked Laura to step inside and wait in the adjoining room while she read for Viv.

This room was cosy and welcoming. Laura laughed to herself to think she'd imagined the whole set up to be spooky, like something out of a horror movie.

The warm atmosphere made her relax and before she knew it, Viv was coming into the room and saying it was her turn. A little hesitantly, Laura went back into the first room to find Frances was seated in the comfy chair with the table in front of her. She had arranged another comfy chair opposite for Laura, so she sat down, not really knowing what to expect.

Frances asked Laura to shuffle the cards, and when she was happy, to place them face down in front of her.

"Relax," she requested of Laura, who attempted to relax and slow down her breathing. Frances began to read for her.

I can see the stars are very important to you," she began. "You hold on to a special message about the stars and it gives you great comfort." Laura caught her breath as Frances continued, "He says whenever you look to the stars, I am there."

Laura fought back the tears. How could this stranger know about this, about how her father had said this to her?

"He is very proud of you," said Frances. "Your mother is not nearby but she constantly thinks about you. She's always there for you and she too holds onto that same message.

I see in the cards that you are working very hard with your studies and you will be extremely successful, top of the class." Laura smiled. She had put so much into her studies, missing out on some of the normal teenage activities. She wanted her parents to be proud of her.

"Your mother's happiness means a lot to you. I can tell you that she will find happiness again, and where she makes her home will be very important to you in the future. A relationship for you will bring unhappiness and feelings of having been let down, but you will be reborn from this experience. I can also tell you that you will find true happiness and fulfilment beyond your wildest dreams." This brought a big smile to Laura's face.

When the reading ended, Laura felt drained but happy. It was only now that many of these messages meant so much to her. She wondered whether the latter part of the reading would be as accurate as the first, when it told of her future happiness. She certainly hoped so.

As she placed the manuscript inside the packing case, she wondered if Kefalos would be the special place referred to by the tarot reader that day. At this moment in time she had little belief that things could get better, and any chance of happiness seemed a long way away. A few years ago she would never have dreamed of what was about to happen or the life she was about to embark on.

As she wondered what was to be her true destiny, the Clock struck and brought her back from her reverie. 'More things to pack,' she thought.

At the bottom of the case was the last remaining item. It was a photograph album stuffed full with photos telling the Story of her life. There were pictures of her christening in the local church, of her first day at school in her new uniform, her skirt too long and her blazer too big on her tiny frame.

There were pictures of family holidays in Anglesey, mountain walks in Wales, several pictures of her with her dad flying a kite, rock pooling and sandcastle building.

She noticed from the photos that there was always a smile on her father's face. How she missed him. There was a picture of her dressed as a little bridesmaid at her sister's wedding, photos of holidays abroad, Christmas festivities and university gigs. There were so many happy memories stored there, and into the cardboard box they went for transportation.

CHAPTER 3
END OF THE AFFAIR

There was a knock on the door. It was the courier who'd arrived to collect the boxes for transportation, some of which were going into storage and the rest transported to Kos, at least for a few months anyway until she got her life back on track.

When the Courier left with the final box, Laura took one last look at the place which had been her home for the past few years. It meant nothing to her now, no sentimental attachment to her whatsoever. She closed the door behind her, thus ending that era of her life and leaving behind the man whom she'd thought loved her. Tomorrow she would fly to Kos to be with her mum. She really needed her right now and felt betrayed by everyone else

Martin had been a vibrant individual at university who seemed to have a lot of friends and acquaintances. Laura was sucked into the various groups, people he spent time with. Martin often left her to fend for herself, eventually returning to her with his beguiling smile and well rehearsed terms of endearment.

Laura began to notice that he seemed to spend more time with other people than he did with her. When she mentioned this, he just laughed and brushed it off. "You are imagining things," he would tell her.

He was always the centre of attention, joking, laughing and entertaining everyone. This was until he and Lara were alone, when he then became somewhat surly and a little bad tempered. At the time it didn't bother her too much, but later she noticed how he changed when he didn't have other people there, no audience to perform to!

He often stayed the night at Laura's flat at the weekends, saying that during the week when he was working, he needed to get a good night's sleep. However, overtime he stayed more and more and they became ardent lovers. Their love making became a feature of each evening and it was eventually decided it would be easier if he moved into the flat permanently. When Martin actually moved into Laura's flat, things had gone well. They stayed home most nights and watched television together cuddled up on the sofa. They made love often and life for Laura seemed good.

After a time they'd decided they were ready to start a family and began preparing for that event. They decorated the spare room in neutral colours, no pink or blue, just a simple white. But as each month passed, Laura became more and more disenchanted with the room and what it represented. It was a hope of them becoming parents, being a family instead of just a couple. But it seemed that no matter how much they wanted it, it just wasn't happening.

She retreated into her shell each month when her period arrived and she knew she wasn't pregnant again, and yet again their dreams had been dashed. Martin became less sympathetic and more verbally abusive, telling her to grow up! But then he began to blame her!

"It's your fault you cannot become pregnant!" he taunted aggressively. He became uncontrollably angry when she suggested they both go and get tested, to try and find out why it wasn't happening. "There's nothing wrong with me!" he insisted indignantly.

Their once wonderful love making became a chore. They filled in charts to trace the best time to conceive. It was clinical, just done to create an outcome and no longer an act of love.

Martin went out more often, while Laura shut down more and more. She was always unhappy and he was always angry. He told her she was stupid. She was a moron who looked a mess and couldn't do anything right. He stated that it was a miracle he came home to such a waste of time! Because of this, she silently cried herself to sleep each night.

She became reluctant to start any conversation with him as it always ending in a row, with words from him that became more and more hateful. Each evening after work she waited for him to start, wondering what it might be tonight. Maybe the dinner was not hot enough, the windows not clean, too many cushions on the couch, some pots left in the sink unwashed! He chose anything at all to start an argument! He would call her stupid, inadequate and thick. For Laura it was like constantly walking on eggshells, always waiting for the next nasty remark.

"I used to think you were intelligent, but not anymore. It's not rocket science!" he accused.

These arguments would give him the opportunity to storm out and leave Laura home alone. It was soul destroying and constant torture for her, but she put up with it, because in spite of everything, she still loved him. Over time she began to feel that maybe she deserved the constant abuse, although this was not what she'd expected when he moved in with her.

She had regressed from a confident and accomplished young woman to a gibbering idiot, as he continually called her. She wondered if he was seeing someone else, as she obviously wasn't what he wanted. She looked at herself in the mirror and hated what she saw. It was her fault all of this. She felt so incredibly low, needing to tell someone about her feelings and suspicions - but who? She couldn't tell her mum, she was living in Greece, and Laura needed the face to face interaction for comfort.

At that moment Laura's phoned bleeped. It was a message received from a fellow former student at university whom she'd remained friends with. She read the message - *just wondering how you are and how life is treating you - would love to see you for a chat'* - And so a meeting was arranged.

As she got ready to meet her friend Carly, Laura felt a little guilty, as if she were betraying Martin by going there with the intention of speaking about him without his knowledge. They met at a little café in town. Carly looked terrific and Laura felt how drab she herself must have looked. After hugs they sat and looked at each other.

"Well then how's things?" asked Carly, to which Laura immediately into burst into tears. "Whatever's wrong?" Carly questioned.

Laura began to relate how she and Martin were having problems. They seemed to be drifting apart, spending little time together. Now, although she found it hard to say to her friend, she suspected he was seeing someone else.

"What makes you think that?" Carly asked caringly. "Have you seen or heard things to have made you feel this way?" Carly hugged Laura closely and told her reassuringly that she was probably mistaken about Martin. It was probably pressures at work which were getting him down. Maybe she was imagining things. Could it be that SHE was the problem?

"Don't do anything silly, and do not over think about things," Laura's friend advised. "All people have ups and downs in their relationships." Carly was adamant that things would get better, but Laura was unsure they would, or could do.

They'd been out for drinks together the night before and Martin had been very attentive and had not criticized her once. At home the next morning he went to the bathroom, and as he did so his phone flashed. It was a number Laura recognised - Carly's number! Laura thought perhaps Carly had messaged Martin to tell him about her meeting with her. That would make him angry, she was sure of that. Laura picked up the phone guiltily and was about to delete the message when she saw the first few words.

'Think she knows something - Be careful!'

All sorts of visions went through Laura's head. So Carly must know something about Martin, but why hadn't she told Laura instead of convincing her it was all in her head? She quickly deleted the message and replaced the phone on the bedside cabinet.

Martin came out of the bathroom, already dressed. "Have to dash. See you later," he said.

"But its Saturday, you're supposed to be having a day off," Laura reminded him.

"Oh, don't start!" he reacted angrily, picked up his jacket and left. Laura sat there, stunned at what had just happened. She made a decision to follow him. Never had she thought she might do this before.

As he left the car park, she ran to her car and quickly fired up the engine. He couldn't have got far and as she rounded the corner she saw him indicating to join the duel carriageway that led into town. There were a few cars in front of her so she held back, hoping he wouldn't see her in his rear-view mirror. She thought he must be going to the office in town, but then he indicated to leave this road and turned off. She left the duel carriageway too but slowed right down so as not to be detected and could see he was now indicating to turn into a housing estate, so she followed tentatively. Eventually he pulled up outside a small-town house.

Laura's heart was now beating madly. 'Who lived here?' she wondered. She watched as he approached the front door and knocked. Laura was shocked when Carly opened the door. She must have arranged to meet Martin and tell him all about what she and Laura had discussed over coffee. Laura sat in the car, unsure of what to do next.

She waited and waited, but when Martin didn't come back out, Laura left the car and walked round the back of the house. She peered in through the window but could see no one in the lounge or kitchen. She tried the back door. It was open, so she crept inside. There was nobody there. Laura listened but could not hear anyone talking, but then she heard a muffled noise coming from the upstairs. She decided she just had to go and see.

Silently she climbed the stairs. From the bedroom, she could hear the sounds of love making. Throwing open the bedroom door, Laura froze on the spot. She could clearly see

43

Carly and Martin naked on the bed. She turned and ran out of the house as quickly as she could. How she got back to her flat she would never know. Her head was swimming. How could he? How could she?

She locked the door behind her; it was still her flat after all. Martin had moved in with her, but it was still hers. She opened the wardrobe door. Here, Martin's shirts and trousers seemed to be standing to attention. Taking the suitcase from the top shelf and in one swift move, she collected all the hanging clothes and dropped them into the case. Next she opened the drawers and removed neatly folded underwear and socks. Into the case she put them.

Now the case was almost full, so was she took a large bin liner and quickly filled it with his shoes and trainers, shorts and t-shirts. This made her realise how little he'd actually accumulated here. Maybe he had a closet full of clothes as Carly's.

After everything she could find that belonged to Martin had been put in bin bags, she opened the front door and carried the case and bags and placed them on the doorstep. As far as she was concerned there was no going back. He'd betrayed her and that was the end of everything.

Her phone began to bleep, it was Martin. She declined the call but it rang again, so she turned if off. She was extremely upset but was also angry too, and this fired her resolve. A while later she heard a key in the front door. He couldn't open it as she'd rotated the mortise lock and had also secured all the windows.

"Laura!" he shouted, but she remained seated on the settee out of view. She knew he wouldn't cause a scene when outside, as that would ruin his respectable image with the neighbours. After gazing up at the window for a little while, he opened the boot of his car and threw all his belongings into it and drove away screeching down the road. Martin was gone!

He never tried to contact her again. This hurt Laura as it made her realise how little she must have meant to him. Had she been just a place to stay when he needed it? There was not much to show for what had originally been a happy relationship. She wondered if Martin would treat Carly the same way he'd treated her. It didn't matter now, as it was finally over. For the first time for her, anger was replaced by tears.

She would have to tell mum because she was putting the flat on the market, as she decided she just couldn't live there anymore. She contacted an estate agent and a solicitor to deal with the sale of the flat and to ensure Martin had no legal right to anything that was in the flat, or the money she would receive from the sale. She took a deep breath and rang mum.

"Hi Mum, fancy a lodger for a few days?" she questioned.

"Oh, darling that would be wonderful," Jenny replied, but then asked, "Are both of you coming?"

Laura couldn't hold it back any longer. Through gulps and stammers she told her mum everything, every last detail. Jenny listened intently to all her youngest daughter had to say, feeling every ounce of the heartache in her daughter's voice. It was decided that as soon as the flat was sold, Laura would go out to Kefalos to be near her mother and to give her time to get over this horrible and tragic period of her life.

The house where Laura was to stay, which had been her mother's house, had been rented out for some while until earlier this year when the tenants had left. It was quite a big house for one person, but Laura didn't mind. Her things had arrived from England and were locked in the basement. She knew some of the things belonging to her mother were still stored here, but there was plenty of room.

Mum had always told her she never wanted to sell the house. Also it was the custom in Greece for the father to

45

provide a home for the daughter, so it had been decided that one day the house should be hers.

It had smelt a little musty when she first unlocked the door and went inside, having been empty for more than three months. Mum had said that was normal and soon remedied by opening all the windows and letting the breeze blow through, along with a few heavily scented air fresheners.

Mum had to go to Kos town, so she'd left Laura to start the job of making it hers. She opened the lounge curtains and took in the view, which from here was quite spectacular. This was one of the reasons her parents had chosen this spot to build their house. The large windows in the lounge overlooked the bay of Kamari, the harbour to the right, with the island of Kastri to the left. The house was on two levels, with a garage and storage area beneath the main part of the house.

A stone staircase with wrought iron banisters led to the main living area of the building, where a dining room with patio window leading to a large Italian tiled balcony was found, along with another splendid view across the entire bay.

Although the interior of the house seemed a little old fashioned to Laura, she was happy to live with it for now. One thing she would not change was the blue and white, 'Cornish Pottery,' lovingly collected over the years and carefully transported from England by Laura's mum. She'd decided to leave it here rather than take it to her new home with Yiannis, as it symbolized the years she'd spent with her husband John, Laura's father. Laura felt comfortable with this pottery, as it reminded her of her childhood years.

Laura busied herself with dusting and sweeping all of the rooms and spraying air freshener everywhere. Just as her mum had suggested, the musty smell was soon gone.

She emptied her cases and then checked the cupboards in the kitchen. Her mother had put basic provisions in there for her, but they would only last a couple of days. Her mother had said she would take her to the large supermarket at the airport to stock up on what she needed. Laura wondered if she should chance a walk into the village or wait till mum came, deciding a little walk would do her good. She could take a look around and get her bearings.

Walking down the track to the main road which led into the village of Kefalos itself, she passed the newly built junior school, the local town football pitch and the beautifully kept cemetery and made a mental note of where the doctor and the dental surgeries were, should she need them in the future.

There were general shops interspersed by tavernas. She noticed hairdressers, a deli, and came across fresh fish being sold from the back of a pickup truck. The local cats were congregating by the truck, lingering close by in the hope of a titbit.

Laura walked into the main square where there were a few eating places, an iron mongers and a bank, although it was now sadly closed. This meant if any banking transactions were needed it meant a trip into Kos town.

She admired the views from the vantage point and then backtracking, she walked up one of the many narrow streets to find a couple of fashion shops and a post office. A Beautiful church was positioned on the right, which Laura quietly crept inside. She thought it magnificent, with its gold decor and coloured icons.

Enough exploration for one morning, she thought, and so returned to the house and took coffee on the balcony at the front of the house. She really enjoyed the view of the bay below, watching the boats come and go and the jet skis as they flew across the water. Speed boats moved rapidly through the waves, towing an inflatable or a water-skier.

It was a really calming and relaxing experience for Laura sitting here, and as she did she thought about what she'd accomplished today, feeling a great sense of achievement. She hoped her stay here would help her recover from the devastating scene she'd witnessed, which had destroyed her life and her confidence.

She made up her mind that after a little rest she would tackle the garden. She thought that after a few hours of hard work, perhaps she would sleep soundly for the first time in ages.

Each day she ventured a little further, increasing her knowledge of the local environment. Other than her responses to the Kalimeras' said to her as people began to recognise her, she didn't enter too much into conversation. However, it did make her realise that the locals were far friendlier here than they were back in England. It seemed that everyone in Laura's home town would just scurry past, barely acknowledging you with maybe the nod of a head.

She still preferred to remain at a distance from people. She was polite, but reserved. Her mind was still confused about what had happened to her. Although she needed to heal from the experience her solitude was not really helping, but it was what she chose.

Her mind cleared a little with each passing day, but the feeling of emptiness and betrayal still remained. Maybe time, along with the Kefalos magic would help. She very much hoped so.

CHAPTER 4
THE HEALING ISLAND

Laura lay on the sun lounger, relaxing in the early morning sun. It was a beautiful Greek morning, where the sky was blue and the air was thick with the wonderful perfumed scent of flowers from the garden. She closed her eyes and all she could hear was the sound of crickets in the bougainvillea trees. No other sound spoilt the tranquillity of the moment and she felt at one with nature.

There was no reason to wear a watch, as time did not matter. She found that her body clock had tuned in with nature. She rose when the sun came up and was ready for bed when the sun went down. The ragged pace of life she'd known before coming to the island seemed a lifetime away.

Just as mum had promised, Kefalos was a special place that healed troubled minds and bodies. It had been hard at first being alone at night in a strange house, but she came to realise that she quite liked her own company with no one to criticise and make her feel stupid. She no longer had to walk on eggshells in case she offended someone, and was no longer subjected to Martin's verbal abuse! She could now make decisions for herself, and because of this, her confidence was growing daily.

Things were getting better and yet things were still not completely right. Her mum had been a rock, always there if she needed her, but stepping back and letting Laura handle things in her own way and plan her own way forward. She was so appreciative of Mum's support, and Yiannis had also helped so much with the legal side of things.

At first she was unsure if she could stay here or whether she would have to return to England, but with each passing week, Kefalos worked its magic. She gradually fell in love with the place and the thought of it becoming her home was becoming a pleasant possibility. She had a big grin on her face when she thought of her mum telling her this would happen.

"I fell in love with Kefalos, and you will too," Mum had told her.

Jenny had insisted her daughter should learn to drive when here on Kos. She'd told Laura that she herself had been nervous at first when she'd come to live here, but said that when the season was over, hardly any shops or cafes were opened in resort.

"If you want to shop for essentials you will have to travel to Kos town to find anything suitable, so owning and driving a car would be a great help, in fact, essential," Laura had advised her daughter.

Jenny said she would sit in the car with her and they would take a little ride along the quieter roads. Although Laura had passed her test and driven in England for a few years by now, she was still quite nervous when she sat in the driving seat of the left hand drive for the first time.

"It's on the wrong side of the car, Mum!" she claimed.

"But you will get used to it very quickly," Jenny laughed.

Laura adjusted the seat and the mirror as instructed and then slowly pulled away. It was fine going along the road until she came to t- junction. She looked both ways just as she would when driving in England, but when Mum said to remember the traffic is on the other side of the road, Laura faltered and stalled the engine! In her mind she was unsure which side of the road she should take when turning right, but it was just a matter of getting used to it.

Within a few days Laura became more relaxed, but was really only driving on the straight main road that led out of Kefalos. Now the roundabouts came and mum tried to explain how the right of way was different to England. Here you had to give way to traffic coming onto the roundabout from the right and not the left.

When she became quite proficient at driving, having tackled the steep windy road to the village and dealing with the mayhem of parked cars, scooters pulling out from everywhere and with tourists walking in the middle of the road without a care in the world, she was ready to drive to Kos town.

Mum warned her about the traffic lights and the crazy way people drove through Zipari. Kos town was an experience and Laura was relieved when they arrived at the big car park just outside the centre.

"Coffee?" her mother suggested.

"To steady my nerves, oh yes," Laura smiled.

"You've done it now, so next time it will be even easier. Just regard everyone else as being an idiot and expect them to do just the opposite from what you would regard as normal and you'll be fine," Jenny gave the instruction.

They stopped for a couple of hours shopping and then returned home.

"So now you need a little run-around of your own," Mum said. "I'll see what Yiannis can sort out for you."

A few days later Yiannis brought her a little ex rental car, fully serviced and ready to go with tax and insurance arranged. It gave Laura a sense of independence, as well as a much needed self-confidence boost. This all helped in getting her back to being herself again.

CHAPTER 5
LIVING AGAIN

Today had been a good day. She'd risen early and had walked down to the harbour. The sea had been like a millpond and she'd tentatively put her toes in the water on Cavos beach. It was cold but didn't chill her feet. She walked slowly into the sea, letting her fingers trail in the water. It was like silk.

No one was around at this early hour, so she gently lowered her shoulders under the water. She felt her body begin to tingle with the coolness. How lucky she was to have this so close to her new home. She lingered for a while, lazily floating and enjoying the gentle caress of the waves. For the first time in months she felt utter contentment.

As she came out of the water she heard a 'beep-beep' from a passing motorcyclist's horn, showing his appreciation for her suntanned and lithe body. She almost felt compelled to wave to the stranger but thought better of it, but still wondered who else was up and about as early as she was.

Drying herself quickly, she decided to walk along the beach road. Nowhere was open yet, so she paused to admire the yachts and catamarans anchored in the bay. A cormorant dipped and dived in the beautiful clear water, catching an early breakfast. Looking back across the bay she could see a couple of small fishing boats leaving the harbour, on their journey to make the catch of the day.

She continued her leisurely stroll along the beach. The clock on the tour shop read six-forty-five and the temperature was already in the seventies. She knew Kefalos market would be opening soon and she'd be able to get a bottle of water and perhaps a fresh croissant.

Her eyes shifted across the bay to the little island with the tiny church. She smiled as she recollected that this was where her mum had married Yiannis a while ago.

Laura was very happy that her mum had found happiness here in Kefalos. It would have been what her dad, John had wanted. It had been his dream to live here, but sadly he'd lost his life and so it wasn't to be. Many times Laura imagined her father was here with her, and often Mum's second husband's ways reminded her of him. Yiannis was a lovely man. She felt she'd known him all her life.

Her walk took her to the ruins opposite the little island of Kastri. Usually this place was swarming with tourists, but this morning there were only a few seagulls resting there before they flew out to sea to follow the fishing boats, hoping the fishermen would throw them some of the smaller fish from their catch.

She took the road up past the large, all-inclusive 'Ikos Hotel' and up to the main road. She strolled up the hill, crossing the road and taking the lane signposted to Kocholari Beach. It was a long trail on foot down there, but she had time to spend. She walked around enjoying the aromas from the fields filled with bright red poppies, looking magnificent as they swayed in the breeze.

Kocholari Beach was so different to Kamari. Here there were waves that could be fierce at times, but the water always seemed slightly warmer here. The shoreline stretched about two kilometres past the kite surfing centre which Laura thought spoilt the look of beach but brought in the tourists. Finally, after about a mile she turned and began the walk back.

Each day Laura wandered around the area, finding new footpaths and new things to see. She found things on her travels that she never knew existed. She was learning to love this place more and more each and every day, as so many others who have fallen for its charm.

Her walk this morning took her through the village past the beautifully restored windmill, which was now a restaurant named, 'Myotopi,' with fantastic views of the island. It had become a top place to visit for tourists coming to Kefalos.

Once out of the village she walked towards the little fishing bay of Limnionis, where around five small fishing boats were moored there in the harbour. This had become her favourite time of day to explore, before the world woke up properly and the tourists filled the beaches and tavernas.

Limnionis consisted of two very different bays, to the left were rocks where the waves here were rough, whilst to the right was found the harbour area which was more sheltered, with the sea here being much calmer.

She sauntered down to the beach area and threw a few tiny stones into the calm water of the bay, watching them skim and jump across the water before finally sinking and being lost forever. Looking to where the boats were moored, she could see the fishermen preparing their nets for the days toil. There were a couple of pickup trucks parked close by, and there she spotted a familiar looking black motorcycle.

She watched as a male figure emerged from one of the boats and climbed onto the motorbike. As he began to climb the steep hill from the harbour, he glanced backwards and saw Laura on the beach below. He cheekily beeped his horn at her and then sped off up the hill. Laura looked up to see the bike going round the first bend and then it was gone from sight. She wondered if it was the same biker she'd seen that early morning a few days before, when she was beeped at when emerging from the sea. She sat for a while on the sand and took in the serenity of the moment.

When she walked down to the harbour on another morning a couple of day later, the sky was overcast and the sea appeared black and menacing. Although it wasn't particularly rough in the harbour, the waves were hitting the roadside wall and cascading water over any passing joggers or cars. Even the little fishing boats seemed reluctant to leave the confines of the harbour this morning.

She decided not to swim this morning, even though she knew the sea would feel warmer. Instead she sat for a while in contemplation, just watching the passing grey clouds and the changing colour of the sea. Maybe if the wind got up, the grey clouds would pass and the sun would shine through. When it did peep through the clouds, it was quite warm.

As Laura watched, more black clouds were gathering overhead and the air pressure was becoming quite oppressive. The wind dropped and everything went still and quiet, but then there was a sudden big gust of wind and the clouds rushed across the sky colliding with each other. The first rumble of thunder echoed over the hills. Now the whole sky was dark and angry, with the sea being black as ink.

Laura saw the first flash of lightning piercing the dark clouds. Picking up her bag she headed for the nearest taverna, reaching it just in time, just as the first large raindrops began to fall. The intensity of the rain increased as she sat watching the storm moving across the horizon, sending purple daggers down towards the sea. It was truly magnificent, yet terrifying at the same time.

The island of Nisyros was no longer in view, as it was completely blanketed in cloud. The rain now was so heavy that it appeared to be like sheets of water spreading across both land and sea. The roads quickly flooded and the water ran down the steep road from the village to the harbour, leaving sand and foliage in its path.

But then, almost as suddenly as it is started, the rain stopped and the sky cleared. A beautiful rainbow appeared over the sea as the sun came shining through from behind the remaining clouds. Within minutes the pavements were dry and tourists began to appear from hotels and apartments. Almost immediately the sun beds and parasols were returned to their rightful position on the beaches, having been moved quickly by the owners when the storm threatened. Again the whole bay of Kamari was bathed in sunshine and it returned to become the pretty resort everyone knew and loved. The smiles returned to the faces of the tourists who'd been disappointed with the weather only an hour ago. They could now laze on the beach and continue to deepen their tans until it was time to return home. Nature was so unpredictable, and no one could control the weather or the seas.

Laura walked back up the hill, carefully avoiding the debris left from the deluge. She went to check on the house to make sure that all was well. Everything felt fresh and clean after the storm, as if all the bad had been washed away. She marvelled at how quickly the weather could change, and how different everywhere looked when the sun wasn't shining. Without sun it sometimes appeared shabby, but when the sun shined on the land, it was pretty and welcoming.

The following day the seaweed dragged in from the seabed by the storms had been removed from the shoreline, the driftwood collected, and so the beaches were once again clean and ready for the tourists.

Laura's confidence was growing and she now felt able to go out alone further afield. She drove to the port of Mastihari and caught the ferry over to the island of Kalymnos. This was once known as a sponge island, as divers from here would collect natural sponges from the sea bed and they'd be sold all over the world, although in their original state they didn't look anything like the creamy coloured sponges available in the shops. Laura was intrigued when she found a little shop in the harbour which had a display of the different types of sponges, along with a replica of the original diving suit used when collecting them.

She found lots of tavernas and fast food eateries dotted around the Harbour area, catering for the short time visitors. A little way back from the harbour were the shops she wanted to visit today to collect some bits and pieces for the house, needing to add her own personality to it.

Feeling artistic she treated herself to some painting materials, small canvases and some pastels, thinking she might experiment and try to catch the atmosphere of the seascapes, as they changed with the passage of time.

She'd taken the fast ferry today which was simply a passenger ferry, the other bigger, but slower ferry, carried vehicles and supplies to and from Kalymnos. With her shopping done, she returned to the port and boarded the ferry. The wind had increased a little and the sea was quite choppy. It didn't bother her but she could see some other passengers were looking a little green around the gills! When the ferry arrived in the port at Mastihari, she disembarked and walked to her car. She was so glad that her mother had made her drive here on the island that time.

The drive home to Kefalos took Laura about twenty minutes. Arriving back at the house, Laura unloaded her shopping and admired some of the items she'd purchased, positioning them on various tables and shelves around the house.

Tomorrow, she thought she might get up early to try and catch the sunrise and attempt to capture the beauty of it,s as it bathed the villages in pink and purple.

CHAPTER 6
MEETING JEANIE

Laura loved to spend the afternoon sitting in one of her favourite bars, the 'Bravo Bar,' just watching the world go by as she looked at the sea, almost hypnotised by the majesty of it.

She would enjoy an ice cold frappé whilst pondering on how much her life had changed over the years, from her carefree childhood living on the moors with her family, along with the dogs and horses, to her university years and the great times she'd had at the beginning of her relationship with Martin. She then remembered the bad times when it all turned sour and had completely devastated her, both emotionally and physically. Now she was able to smile contentedly to herself. She was now in good physical shape and more emotionally stable. At long last she'd started to get her life back on track.

The Bravo Bar was busy today and most of the seats inside were taken. Deep in her thoughts, Laura was woken from her reverie by a quiet voice asking," May I sit at this table please?" Laura looked to see a young woman whom she'd seen in here a few times before, also always on her own. They'd nodded to each other before in recognition, but had never actually spoken.

"Of course, please do," Laura invited in a pleasant tone.

"I'm not disturbing you am I," the lady questioned. "I've often seen you sitting on your own in here."

Yes," Laura accepted. "Always on my own," she smiled. Laura thought the young woman was pretty, with her flame red hair and freckles.

"My names Jeanie, by the way," the lady announced, introducing herself.

"I'm Laura."

The waitress came and Jeanie also ordered a frappé for herself and another for Laura, who by now felt very comfortable in her presence.

"Do you live here on the island?" she asked Jeanie.

"Yes, I've been living here for about six years," Jeanie returned. "I am married to a Greek man named Yiannis."

"My mum is married to a Greek man called Yiannis," Laura told Jeanie. "She moved here a few years ago, just after my dad died."

Laura thought this was amazing. Here she was telling a complete stranger about her personal life, yet it felt okay, as if she'd known this lady for a long time.

"Are you married?" Jeanie asked.

"No," Laura replied with honesty. "I was in a relationship and had planned to get married, but it never happened."

"Sorry, I'm being too nosey," Jeanie stated, a little embarrassed.

"No, its fine," Laura replied, trying her best to reassure her new friend. "We met at uni, had a great time, moved in together and were trying for a family but it didn't happen. He blamed me for the lack of pregnancy and we drifted apart. He then found somebody else - end of story."

"I'm sure there is a lot more to it than that," Jeanie remarked.

"Yeah, a lot of tears and lots of anger, plus being made to feel stupid by a so-called friend," Laura admitted.

"So that's what brought you to Kefalos?" Jeanie said, more like a statement than a question.

"My mum says this place heals everything," Laura confided. "I guess I'm on the mend now."

The time flew by, with each learning snippets of the others life and how Kefalos had helped them. Jeanie told Laura how she'd come here as a holiday rep, and as many

59

others had done before she'd fallen in love with the island of Kos.

Jeanie had met Yiannis at the end of one long hot summer, when she was sunbathing in the autumn sun and she'd watched him fishing from the shore. Yiannis had almost caught her beach towel when he was casting his line. He told her how sorry he was that he'd almost hooked her and they'd both laughed at the double meaning of this.

Jeanie and Yiannis had sat chatting all that afternoon and agreed to meet again that evening. Their relationship blossomed and they were married the following summer, making their home in the village.

Jeanie's phone rang. She answered the call and carried on a sharp short conversation in Greek.

"That was my Greek mother-in-law," she told Laura, after ending the call abruptly. "She can't understand why I like to sit here most afternoons looking at the sea. I must go home now, I have been summoned! Laura, I have really enjoyed chatting with you today." Laura smiled.

"Let's do it again soon," they both blurted out at the same time, making them laugh. It had been a long while since Laura had laughed like this.

"Do you know the Corner Café?" Laura questioned.

"Of course," Jeanie replied. Instantly Laura felt a little stupid. Of course she knew the 'Corner,' she'd lived here for six years!

"Shall we meet there?" Laura questioned.

"That would be great. When and what time?" her new friend asked.

"Maybe Friday afternoon, at about two," Laura suggested.

"Sounds good to me," Jeanie confirmed, and they did meet up on the following Friday afternoon as arranged.

Laura had met up with Jeanie several times now for coffee, with the two becoming very good, firm friends.

60

They'd learned a lot about each other's lives and really enjoyed their girlie times together.

CHAPTER 7
NIKOS

Laura continued to enjoy her early morning walks. This morning when she reached the harbour, there were several yachts anchored in Cavos Bay. As usual she was on her own at this early hour but really enjoyed being alone down here on the beach; the solitude before everyone else invaded the sand, to her was Heaven. She sat on one of the sun beds and looked out at the sea. There was a slight breeze and the sun caught the small waves and made them sparkle and glisten.

The pleasure boats taking tourists on daily trips to Nisyros, the volcanic island visible from Kamari bay and various other islands, were being made ready by the owners. One of the yachts in the bay was predominantly black, almost appearing like mirrored glass. As it turned and bobbled in the sea it appeared to change colour from black to metallic grey and then silver.

She watched as a small dinghy left the yacht and travelled across to the harbour. A male figure alighted on the quayside. Laura thought it must be a holidaymaker coming for supplies. The figure disappeared behind the anchored trip boats.

Laura turned to look at the road behind her to see a black motorbike ridden by a figure dressed all in black, from black boots to a black helmet. The bike was also shiny black, just like the yacht. Soon the motorbike was gone and Laura was left wondering who the rider was, but as usual it was only a momentarily fleeting thought.

Later in the day, when she met her friend, Jeanie made a suggestion. "Laura, do you fancy an evening out tonight?" she questioned. "We could go for something to eat and a couple of drinks. There's a group playing at the Sydney Bar I think you might enjoy."

"That sounds like fun," admitted Laura.

"Yes," said Jeanie. "And Yiannis will be there, so you can meet him and a few of his workmates."

Laura hesitated when hearing this. Maybe it sounded too much like the real-world, meeting other people and being out at night.

"I'm sure you'll enjoy it," Jeanie said, picking up on Laura's hesitation. Laura reluctantly agreed and they made the necessary arrangements.

Laura was feeling a little sick at the thought of going out tonight. She'd been sheltered here, doing things at her own pace and not relying too much on other people. Her only outings had been alone on long walks around the resort in the early hours each day. She didn't have a lot of contact with strangers, and was reluctant to begin.

She showered and dried her hair. The sun had added blonde streaks to her normally dark hair and her time in the sun had left her with a lovely tan. She really was a beautiful girl, but she did not have the confidence to see this. All the self-belief she'd previously had had been taken away by Martin. Feeling good about herself had no longer been on the agenda, not since he'd robbed her of her confidence and self-worth with his constant criticism.

She worked her way through her wardrobe discarding dresses that were inappropriate, either too short or too flashy. She finally settled on a not too short strappy black dress that showed off her trim figure and glorious tan. After applying just a trace of lipstick and mascara, she was ready.

The butterflies in her stomach now had clogs on, as she walked down the hillside to the harbour road and then along the seafront to Sydney's. She'd eaten here before with her mother and knew the food was excellent.

As she arrived she noticed most of the tables were occupied by tourists enjoying their evening meal. She walked through to the bar area and perched on one of the stools in front of the long bar. Laura felt a little conspicuous sitting there on her own, so it came as a great relief to her when Jeanie arrived with Yiannis. Introductions were made and she began to relax a little.

"Nikos and maybe Costas will be joining us soon, so we need to get a table for five," Yiannis instructed.

Jeanie leaned over and whispered in Laura's ear. "You look fabulous girl" she said.

"Thanks, but I'm a little nervous," Laura admitted.

"Don't be. Let's just enjoy ourselves and have some fun," Jeanie advised.

They found a table and the three of them sat down. The waiter came and they ordered drinks, at least she could have a drink to steady her nerves as she'd left the car back at the house.

"Yas Nikos," Yiannis shouted, looking up at the new arrival.

Laura looked to see a tall dark-haired Greek man heading directly to the table, firstly kissing Jeanie on both cheeks and then warmly hugging Yiannis.

"This is Laura," Jeanie announced.

"Very pleased to meet you," Nikos expressed. He extended his hand towards Laura and looked straight into her eyes. Laura immediately felt herself blush. This man was gorgeous!

"At last we meet, my little lonesome lady," Nikos said, almost purring. Laura frowned at him, obviously confused. "I have passed you many times and waved to you," Nikos explained, but Laura still looked confused as he continued, "I am the rider on the motorbike. I see you at the beach at the harbour at Limnionis."

Laura realised it was the black motorbike rider who'd been beeping at her. "Oh yes," she said shyly.

"I saw you from the boat yesterday," Nikos smiled. Laura thought about it, deciding it must have been him she'd seen in the dingy leaving the yacht and heading for the harbour. "I was doing a little work on the yacht," he added.

Laura nodded in acknowledgement. She remembered that Jeanie had told her that Yiannis worked with Nikos.

Nikos sat with them and they ordered from the menu. As usual the food was delicious, with the conversation being even better, being both lively and full of laughter. A little later the group began their performance, playing many well known songs. Everyone joined in singing and dancing along with them.

Time passed so quickly and it was soon getting late. The live music had finished, with the band completing their second set of the evening and all four had enjoyed it. Nikos had paid Laura a lot of attention throughout the evening and she felt quite at ease in his company. She had to admit that despite previous reservations, she had really enjoyed the evening immensely but it was now time to go. She began to think about the trek back to the house.

"I think it's time I made tracks," she said.

Nikos looked quite disappointed. He felt a definite attraction for Laura and had really enjoyed the evening, not really wanting it to end. "Do you live far from here?" he asked.

"Just a little out of the village," Laura confided. "It's only a short walk."

"Just a short walk to the village," Nikos stated. "No, Laura, that road up there is dark and lonely at night." Laura had never thought of it that way, but she'd never walked up that road after dark. "I will take you" Nikos offered.

Laura didn't want to insult him but she declined his offer, as she knew that like her, he had drunk several glasses of red wine.

"I will walk with you." Nikos suggested. Laura tried to hide her surprise at this statement. It was a bit of a long walk even though she'd previously said it wasn't, but with Nikos for company, it would be safer for her not to walk alone in the dark. And after all, Jeanie had assured Laura that Nikos was a good man who would take care of her.

After saying their goodbyes, Laura walked down the steps at Sydney's with Nikos. Looking back, she noticed the staff there watching her leave. She felt a little embarrassed that they might think she shouldn't be going home with someone she'd only just met. They walked slowly along the seafront in the moonlight which lit up the night sky, barely speaking as they walked up the steep winding road towards the village. When they reached the top of the incline, Laura turned to Nikos.

"I'm almost home now," she said. "It was so kind of you to walk this far with me but I'm safe now. Thank you."

"So, you live near here?" Nikos asked.

"My mother's house is just a short walk from here," Laura returned.

"Your mother's house, oh I see," Nikos remarked, sounding a little disappointed. Laura wasn't sure what he meant, but she thanked him again and turned to walk away.

"Can we meet again soon?" Nikos asked.

Laura's stomach was strangely full of butterflies. She'd found this man really attractive as well as being a lovely person to chat with, but was she ready to accept an invitation from him? Her trust in men had been smashed and she was unsure if she wanted to open herself to the possibility being hurt again.

"Maybe we could go swimming tomorrow morning," Nikos suggested, not wanting to concede defeat.

This sounded quite safe to Laura, so she replied, "It's a date."

Instantly she thought about having used the word, 'date.' She wasn't a young teenager anymore; she was a grown woman going on 'a 'date.'

Nikos walked away from her and began the trek down to the harbour, but instead, he walked towards the village. Laura crossed the road and walked up the little track that led to her mother's house. Looking back, she saw he was now out of sight, which made her feel strangely sad. Reaching the house, she unlocked the door and went inside. All sorts of thoughts were swimming around in her head. He was a good-looking man, that she knew, but she didn't really know anything else about him except that he worked with Yiannis on boats. Perhaps at their next meeting she would learn a little more.

One thing she knew for certain was that she was looking forward to seeing him again, and a little flutter in her stomach made her gasp, which confirmed this. Was she being silly, thinking this brief encounter could lead anywhere? She climbed into bed and cuddled her pillow. It would be nice she thought to have something more than a cushion to cuddle.

With her last thoughts before sleep being of Nikos, with a broad smile on her face, she drifted off to sleep.

CHAPTER 8
GETTING TO KNOW YOU

Laura saw Nikos leaning against his motorbike in the harbour where they'd agreed to meet there. As she arrived and approached him, he stood up to greet her. When she reached him, he opened his arms, engulfed her in a bear hug and then kissed her on both cheeks. Laura was a little surprised at this action, but then she remembered this was the normal greeting for the Greeks'.

"Come. We will go to the beach so we can swim, relax and get to know each other," Nikos said, gesturing towards a small dingy moored between two fishing boats, which Laura gingerly climbed into. Nikos started the outboard motor and with a 'put-put-put' sound, they quickly left the confines of the harbour and motored out towards the black yacht anchored in the middle of the bay. Nikos manoeuvred the dingy alongside and climbed up the ladder.

"This is the yacht you were working on the other day," Laura remarked. "Will the owner not mind us being on it?"

"I think not," Nikos replied, so Laura decided it must be okay.

With a helping hand from Nikos, she boarded the yacht. It was luxurious, with white leather seats contrasting fabulously with the black décor elsewhere. Nikos told Laura to get comfortable while he went into the engine house and fired up the engine. He then raised the anchor and they were soon sailing across the bay towards the headland, which they rounded and travelled for a little while longer until coming upon a sandy cove. Sheer cliffs surrounded this place, showing that this beach could only be reached by boat.

Nikos cut the engine and dropped the anchor. It was relatively sheltered here and the water was quite calm. He told Laura it was safe to swim ashore from here. She took off her t shirt and shorts to reveal a small black bikini. Nikos watched her undress and sighed in appreciation of her lovely body. He took off his polo shirt and shorts, making Laura take a sharp intake of breath at the sight of his six-pack. It was as though they'd both received a memo that morning informing them of a dress code for the day as Nikos also sported black swimming trunks, which showed off his tanned muscular frame.

"You like black," she laughed.

"You too," he said, gesturing towards her attire. Laura felt relaxed and happy in his company, which was unusual for her.

"Race you to the shore!" Nikos shouted diving into the water and getting a head start. Without hesitation, she instantly dived in after him.

Both were strong swimmers, Laura's mum, Jenny, had made sure of that after her own ordeal in the sea when she'd nearly drowned. They matched each other stroke for stroke, until they reached the shallow water where a draw was declared. There were a few pebbles before the sand and Nikos held out his hand to help steady her.

There had been no thoughts of towels when they'd jumped off the yacht, so they sat directly on the sand with knees tucked in their arms. Sitting in silence, they gazed at the sea whilst getting their breath back.

The yacht bobbed up and down in the gentle waves as the sun beat down upon them. The only sound was that of the waves as they gently shifted the pebbles on the shoreline. With no one in sight, only the two of them, they sat in silence for some time, neither speaking, just soaking in the serene atmosphere of this beautiful place.

"I think I'm in love," Laura said quietly.

"You have a boyfriend, a husband?" Nikos asked, looking at her.

"No Nikos. I am in love with this island," she informed him, whilst gently smiling at his misunderstanding.

"I love this island very much too," he said. "Have you come to stay with your mother for a holiday?"

"I will tell you how I came to be here, Nikos, because I believe you should know the person I have become," Laura said, making her companion change his expression to that of confusion.

Slowly she related the story of the loss of her much-loved father, her university years, her mother's marriage to a Greek man from this island, her unhappy relationship with Martin and her discovery of him in bed with her best friend and her feelings of betrayal and utter worthlessness.

Nikos did not interrupt, but sat quietly next to her. When she stopped talking, he placed his hand caringly on her shoulder to offer comfort. She turned face him and in his eyes she saw caring and compassion, more than she'd never seen from Martin. She edged forward and kissed him gently on the cheek.

"Thank you for listening, Nikos," she said.

"Thank you for sharing this with me," he replied. They stood in unison and put their arms around each other, staying in this embrace for several seconds.

"I must get the yacht back now," Nikos said, breaking the clinch.

"Of course," Laura agreed. "You wouldn't want to take advantage of the owner." Nikos smiled.

He took her hand as they paddled into the sea and then swam back to the yacht and climbed onboard. Just as before, Nikos expertly piloted the boat back to the bay and anchored up and then took them back to the harbour in the dingy.

Laura thought it had been a lovely morning. "When will the owner be back?" she asked

"I think very soon," Nikos smiled.

"Well at least I can say I have been on a luxury yacht once in my life," she laughed and Nikos smiled.

70

He really liked this young woman and wondered how long she would stay here in Kefalos. He hoped to have enough time for him to persuade her to stay forever, perhaps.

Back in the harbour they said goodbyes and Nikos climbed onto his motorbike. He was about to leave, but before he did he shouted to Laura, "Can you come out to play tonight?" he said jokingly like a teenager. "There are things I have to tell you."

Laura was intrigued. "I can meet you at Corner café," she said.

"Okay, about eight?" he questioned.

"Eight will be great," she smiled. And with that said, Nikos was gone.

Later she reminisced about the day she'd just had. Unbelievable! She'd spilled her heart out to someone she'd only just met or hardly knew, in fact she knew nothing about Nikos, nothing at all!

Nikos in turn had said he had things he must tell her. She wondered what they might be, perhaps he was married, had children, or both! What a fool she'd been not to ask him. A good-looking man as he was simply must be married or in a long-term relationship. He was polite and courteous, as well as being full of fun and laughter. Yes, the day had been enjoyable and she'd felt totally at ease with him.

She knew he worked on the boats; perhaps he was a carpenter, or a mechanic who serviced the engines on the yachts. He'd listened politely to her when she'd told him her story, but she really didn't give him a chance to say much about himself, or perhaps he didn't want to say much about his present situation.

She felt a little foolish and selfish, thinking it had all been about her. Well tonight she decided she'd find out all about Nikos, but she hoped she wouldn't be disappointed.

She showered, dried her hair and applied cream to her slightly burnt shoulders, burned from sitting still in the sun on the beach, and helped by the salty sea air when on the boat. Selecting a short black and white sixties style shift dress from the wardrobe she put it on, and after admiring herself in the full length mirror, she made her way to corner café.

As she passed, she noted that all the sun beds were folded and the beach was empty. Although it was still relatively light she knew it would be dark very soon, as darkness fell suddenly here in Greece. There was no gradual transition here, no measured twilight as in England.

Arriving at the bar, Laura spotted a row of motorbikes parked outside. There were usually more than this parked during the day, and at weekends a local bikers group stopped here for coffee.

She sat at a table nearest the sea and was deep in thought when a roar went up from the bikers. Laura turned to see Nikos being greeted by the bikers. He looked stunning in white t shirt and black jeans. He came to her table and before seating himself, he greeted her with the customary kiss on both cheeks.

At the time Laura was drinking a frappé, so Nikos ordered the same. When the barman brought it to the table he greeted Nikos like a long-lost friend. It seemed to Laura that everyone knew her date.

"Watch him, he's dangerous," the barman joked, to which Laura raised her eyebrows. Nikos play punched him on the arm and then moved his chair closer to Laura. She shifted a little, feeling slightly uncomfortable being so close to him, given that he may be married.

"Did you enjoy yourself today?" he asked.

"I really did, especially the luxury of the private sail on such a beautiful yacht. I bet it cost a lot of money, way out of my league. But it was very nice to live the life of the rich and famous for a day." Nikos laughed as Laura said this.

"We could go again if you want to," he said.

"I don't think we should risk it again," she replied. "The owner may not be pleased about his workman making use of his beautiful yacht."

"Come on," Nikos laughed, "let's live dangerously." Laura laughed with him.

Suddenly his expression changed. He now sported a more serious look on his face. "You told me your story, now I will tell you mine," he began. Laura listened intently as he told her about himself.

"My family have lived in Kefalos for many, many years. My family was well known here for having a family business here on the island. As a child, I lived here with my parents and grandparents. I had many friends and enjoyed a happy childhood living on this beautiful island.

I played on the beaches and swam in the sea almost daily. I went to school in the village and then the senior school in Antimachia, working hard at my studies and getting good results, which allowed me to apply for a place at university.

Before joining the family business I went to university in England, where I studied business management, finance and political studies. When I returned to Kos, I was supposed to learn the family business from my father and his brother. Dad and my uncle were partners in the business.

There was a terrible accident when I was young in which both my parents, along with my uncle, were killed. My uncle was childless and as the only son of my parents, I was sole heir to the family business. So at the tender age of twenty-two, I became the outright owner of the company." Nikos spoke quietly, and Laura could hear the grief in his voice as he continued.

"My grandmother took me under her wing and taught me the things I had to know about respect for myself and for other people, especially for those who worked for the company. Meanwhile I learned the trade from the workforce, the very people who now worked for me. The company was and still is very successful and I have enjoyed a good life from it. Now at the tender age of thirty I have accomplished much, of which I am very proud.

I have a great workforce and they all seem to be happy to work for me, although I never say they work FOR me, I always say they work WITH me. For this reason, I am more than content with my working life." He paused while Laura looked at him.

"So your company works on boats?" she questioned.

"Well, kind of," he smiled. "My company builds boats. More specifically we build luxury yachts."

"Like the one you were working on the other day when I saw you?" Laura queried.

"Well let's just say that we build yachts that only the extremely rich and famous can afford," Nikos confirmed.

"Would that black one be one of those?" she asked, now well drawn into the story.

"Not quite," he replied. "Have you seen the ones in Kos harbour, or those that anchor offshore here in the bay, the ones that have their own helipads? Many of those in these waters are built, and fitted by my company."

Laura sat in stunned silence, as the reality of who her companion actually was. Finally she found the words to ask, "So, you own this company?" Nikos nodded. "Just YOU alone own the company?" He nodded again. "And the yacht you were working on?"

"It's mine," he told her. "I own it!" Laura was speechless.

"So, you must be pretty well off, I mean wealthy," she said. Nikos nodded again. "And you don't mend boats?" He shook his head. "And Yiannis works for you?"

"He is one of my customer service team," Nikos stated.

"Wow! You certainly did have things to tell me!" Laura said, really stunned by what he'd revealed to her. "And there is no one who shares this opulent life with you?" was her final question. Nikos smiled as he knew what she was asking. Laura waited for the answer with bated breath.

"Not as yet, but I have some dreams that maybe one day someone will want to live with me and have a family, so I can pass on my success to my children." She was happy when hearing this.

Laura thought of the lifestyle money can buy, and the rich and famous people who Nikos must come into contact with, each and every working day.

She thought that with his good looks and physique he would be looking to marry a supermodel or a movie star, or some such beautiful celebrity. She looked at Nikos and he returned the look, staring back at her and cocking his head inquisitively.

"Well?" he asked finally.

"Well what?"

"Have I upset you telling you this?" he asked with genuine concern.

"You have completely blown my mind!" she began. "I thought you were a mechanic who mended boats, just some guy that rode a motorbike who liked to watch live bands and enjoyed a drink with his friends."

"But that IS who I am!" he retaliated.

"But you must be very rich?" Laura stated.

"Does that really matter? Financially, yes I am, but in many others – no," he stated, but then threw her with his question. "Did you like me when you thought of me as the boat mechanic?" Laura gasped a little at this direct question. She had grown quite fond of him in such a short time, even when not knowing about the wealth.

"Well yes," she admitted.

"Then why is it different now?" he pleaded. "I am the same person you met this morning. I like you a lot Laura and want to spend more time with you. Please tell me you want the same."

Laura was flabbergasted. She'd never been happier on this island than when she was with him, but would she have felt the same about Nikos if she'd she known exactly WHO he was.

She looked at the other people in 'Corner café.' Some seemed to be looking in their direction whilst others were oblivious to her and the super rich man accompanying her.

"You have gone very quiet Laura," Nikos said a little sadly. "Have I made you unhappy?"

"No," she replied."It's just a lot to take in."

"Please Laura," he said softly. "I'm just a guy sitting beside you, asking you to like me and spend time with me - Nothing more and nothing less. Can you be that girl, Laura?"

"Yes Nikos," Laura smiled. "Yes, I can."

CHAPTER 9
LEARNING TO LOVE AGAIN

"Tonight," Nikos announced, "I will take you to eat in a beautiful restaurant. We will get to know each other better and maybe if the stars align, we will fall in love."

Laura gasped at the thought of falling in love. She knew she was already well on the way to falling in love with Nikos, but now that she knew about his wealth, she was afraid people would call her a gold digger! Maybe they would think she was only after him for his money, especially with her being a foreigner and only a visitor to the island. So many thoughts were running through her mind and her head was spinning!

Nikos had taken Laura on trips to many parts of the island which she'd never seen before. He drove her over the mountain road from Kardamena to Pyli, with its magnificent views of the salt lakes in Tigaki and the coastline of Turkey.

She marvelled at the harsh volcanic landscape as they sped along the high winding road past a quarry where granite had been mined for many years. He took her to the mountain village of Zia, with its quirky stalls and tavernas.

Nikos was very knowledgeable about the island, which was hardly surprising as it had been his home for thirty years. He began to relate to Laura the history he'd been told by his grandma. There were numerous historical places he'd taken her to see, like the Asklepion, the outdoor hospital in Kos Town. This was the world's first, so oldest hospital ever built to treat people. It was also the place which gave birth to the phrase, 'Hippocratic Oath,' as legend has it that the man, Hippocrates himself, was supposed to have sat down with his medical pupils and given them instruction.

Laura and Nikos had swum together on many occasions and sunbathed on many of the beautiful beaches dotted around the shoreline during their frequent sailings around the island.

"Today we are going to do something completely different," Nikos told Laura.

"And what would that be?" she asked, intrigued.

"Wait and see. Do you have any denim jeans?" he questioned, confusing her even more.

Laura looked at him and cocked her head on one side. "Why would I need to wear jeans today when it's so very hot?" she questioned.

"Okay," Nikos conceded. "Put your swimwear on underneath, but please put on your jeans and trainers." Although Laura didn't have any idea what this was about, she still complied with his request.

She went to meet him as usual at the harbour, but as she could not see him anywhere, she sat waiting on the wall and looked out to sea. The waves were rough today and there was a strong wind, so very characteristic of this island. While she waited, she tried to figure out why Nikos had asked her to wear jeans and trainers. It was a conundrum to her, as it was still very hot with the Greek sun being quite fierce.

Nikos arrived on his black motorbike, complete with a second crash helmet on his arm. He got off the bike and opened the box on the back of it, took out a small leather jacket and passed it to Laura. "Please put this on," he requested. "Today you're going to learn to ride with me," he said. "If you enjoy it, we will buy you your own safety gear today." Laura was a little hesitant as she'd always been afraid of motorbikes.

After donning the jacket, she climbed gingerly onto the seat and securely fastened the helmet on her head, double checking it for tightness.

"Put your arms around my waist," Nikos instructed.

"That's easy," she laughed nervously, nuzzling into his back.

"I'll take it slowly," he reassured her, setting off along the Harbour road. As they reached the first bend and were about to round it, Nikos instructed, "Lean with me, Laura, don't try to stay upright all the time."

As they joined the main road, she was still feeling nervous. They climbed the hill and Laura allowed herself a couple of seconds to glance at the island of Kastri as they passed. Now that they were on a straight piece of road Nikos accelerated, making Laura cling on for dear life!

They stayed on the main road until they reached the airport roundabout, and there Nikos turned and headed back in the direction of Kefalos. Laura, a little reluctantly began to relax, and had to admit that she was beginning to enjoy the ride. When they returned to the harbour, Nikos stopped the bike and they both got off.

"Well how was that?" he questioned.

"Frightening," she laughed, "but enjoyable. I felt safe with you though."

"Okay we can go a bit further tomorrow," he advised and then made a suggestion. "Now let's go for a swim."

They swam at Cavos beach. There were only a few tourists there today so they stayed in the refreshing cool sea for a while.

"Come," he said later, offering her his hand, "I will take you home."

Laura climbed back on the bike again, but this time feeling a little more confident. Instead of going up the normal road past the harbour, Nikos drove down the road past the 'Golden Fleece' restaurant. Laura had not been up this way before. After negotiating many twists and turns and steep climbs they came out next to the 'Anthoula Hotel' and onto the main road to the village.

Nikos manoeuvred his way skilfully through the parked cars in the village and dropped Laura on the road close to her home. After goodbyes were said, they arranged to meet the next day and maybe go a little further on the bike, visiting a few more remote places.

"Hey Laura, I have an idea," Nikos suddenly announced. "Would you like to come with me on the Sunday ride this weekend?"

He explained that she would be welcome to join him on the Sunday outing with the other bikers from the club. Laura agreed and this became a regular event for her each weekend from then on. She got to know other female riders in the club and really enjoyed the exhilaration of the fast drives around the island.

Laura was enjoying being with Nikos more and more. He seemed to surprise her everyday with trips out and stories of his family. His caring ways made her feel safe, and the hurt she'd been feeling before coming to Kos was beginning to vanish. They were spending more and more time together and it was obvious to all that they were now very much in love.

How magical the sea looked this evening. They walked barefoot along the water edge. The moon cast its long shadows across the water and the waves shimmered. Holding hands they walked along in silence, not speaking as if it might spoil the magic if they disturbed the silence.

Coming to a halt under a tree, Nikos pulled Laura into his arms and kissed her. "I love being with you, Laura," he confessed. "You have completely changed my life and I know I'm falling in love with you." Laura smiled, feeling the same way about him.

She said nothing in return; instead she kissed him firmly on the lips as he held her tightly in his arms. They were both so happy in this moment, both knowing they'd found someone very special. Life for the both of them, felt good.

Laura decided it was time Nikos met her mother and Yiannis, and so one late afternoon they drove down the long and winding road past the many little churches dotted here and there. Signposts directed tourists to various beaches along the road, and they passed a restaurant built close to the beach. Here they took a dirt track that eventually led them to her mother and Yiannis's property. Nikos thought the location of the house, perched above a small cove and hidden behind an outcrop of gorse bushes was fantastic.

They were welcomed with hugs and kisses. Yiannis immediately recognised Nikos when he saw him. He hadn't realised when Laura had spoken of her new man that it was this particular Nikos she'd been speaking about. He'd known Nikos from when a young boy, as well as his parents, Dimitris and Katarina. He'd shared in the shock and grief with the entire village when they were killed in the tragic accident.

He'd seen Nikos grow from a small boy living in Kefalos, into the man he was today. He knew his character and was so pleased that he'd found happiness with Laura. Likewise he was very happy that it seemed Laura had found happiness with Nikos. He hoped the relationship between the two would blossom, just as his and Jenny's had when they'd found each other and helped each other to get over the loss of their respective partners.

"You should go down there to the cove," Yiannis told the couple, but particularly Laura. "It's a magical place where your mother and father used to come. I also used to take my first wife, Eleni there," he then paused for a moment and they could all see him becoming emotional as he revealed, "This is where your mother saved my life."

"Come Laura," Nikos smiled. "Let's go and take a look."

Jenny and Yiannis watched Nikos and Laura as they climbed down the steep slope to the cove below, holding hands as they walked along the soft sand and paddled in the calm water.

Yiannis put his arm around Jenny. "It will work its magic for them too, I'm sure," he said kissing Jenny. When they looked down to the cove, Nikos was holding Laura in the same embrace and kissing her.

Later, as they sat on the porch, and as the sunset painted the sea and sky a deep orange, happiness and contentment reigned. "Magic - pure magic," Nikos beamed, at which Laura smiled.

Nikos truly loved this island and his enthusiasm was contagious. Laura loved all the places they'd visited, but most of all her heart belonged to Kefalos. This place and its people had helped her recover from all those bad times she'd experienced.

They sat in the restaurant which overlooked the sea and watched silently as the moon was reflected along the waves. It certainly was a fantastic view and very romantic. Although they'd spent much time together, they had not yet made love. Even though their bodies were telling them to do so, both had an element of reluctance. Laura was afraid of getting hurt again. She'd thought Martin would be her soul mate forever, and Nikos was afraid to move things too quickly, knowing how hurt she'd been in her previous relationship. He wanted to gain her trust and affection and not spoil their relationship by moving things too quickly.

As they held hands across the table they gazed into each other's eyes, both with a yearning to make this relationship work, although both in their own way, nervous and afraid.

The meal was delicious. They both sighed with contentment at exactly the same moment. "I think it's time we headed home, don't you?" Nikos questioned, after they'd both consumed a coffee and brandy.

"What a good idea," Laura replied, with a wicked look in her eyes. "Would you like to come in for a coffee?" she questioned Nikos after the drive back to where she lived.

"Will your mother not mind?" Nikos questioned, quite naively, Laura thought. She'd never told him that, although it was her mother's house, Jenny didn't actually live there anymore. She thought he would have known that her mother lived in the house with Yiannis, and didn't just visit him from time to time. But then she remembered how she thought the yacht they'd first sailed on had belonged to someone else, so she could see and understand his mistake.

"I'm sure she won't mind," she said, smiling to herself. Laura turned the key in the lock and opened the door. "Shush, "she said with her finger on her lips, "we don't want to wake anyone," she teased. She took him by the hand and led him to the lounge. "Come in and get comfortable," she invited.

Nikos sat down but didn't look particularly at ease. Laura threw off her shoes and snuggled up to him on the settee. He put his arm gently around her shoulders and she gazed into his eyes.

"Make love to me," she purred.

Nikos gasped, "But your mother," he pleaded.

"Is about five kilometres away in her own house with Yiannis," she explained. "This used to be hers, but she doesn't live here anymore."

"So, there is no one else here?" he queried.

"Just us, you and me," Laura smiled. "Now - Kiss me."

Nikos was happy to oblige. She was so beautiful. He manoeuvred her body into position. He'd thought about this moment many times before, and was now both nervous and excited in equal measures at what was to come. He'd so wanted to make love to her on so many occasions.

Laura held out her hand. "Come with me," she invited, leading Nikos to her bedroom. One small light illuminated the room. It was perfect.

"Are you sure?" Nikos asked, as though seeking a final permission.

"I have never been more sure of anything in my life," she smiled.

They looked at each other like two teenagers. Laura blushed, Nikos coughed, but then he put his arms around her, picked her up and laid her on the bed. Frantically they removed each other's clothes, both hungry for what was about to happen.

Nikos was gentle, caring only for Laura's feelings. Martin had never been like this, in fact he'd been totally opposite, not caring about Laura's feelings or needs but only wanting to satisfy himself!

Nikos gently kissed her body, caressing every inch. Slowly he moved his body over hers. Their breathing was fast and Laura couldn't stop herself moaning out loud. Ever so gently he entered her and their bodies became entwined. Two became one.

Never had Laura felt so loved, so wanted, and so complete. It was wonderful. This was how lovemaking should always be.

When both satisfied, they lay in each other's arms for a while. "I should go," Nikos said, although more of a question than a statement of intent.

"Stay," Laura said, whilst drawing circles in the hairs on his chest

"But what will people say?" he argued.

"They would say that I am the luckiest girl in the world to have you," she beamed.

"Are you sure you want me to stay?" She answered his question with a kiss.

"I think your body is telling you that you are not quite ready to leave – yet," she teased.

Nikos looked down at the tell tale sign his body was telling him. He looked at Laura and gave her a cheeky, knowing grin. They then made love to her again.

"Now your body is ready to relax," Laura joked, as they both lay there exhausted, but satisfied.

Early the next morning, before leaving the house Nikos told Laura he had to go to Athens later that day for business, but would be back in a few days. She reluctantly let him leave the house and then snuggled back under the duvet, now feeling more content and happier than she'd ever done in her life.

CHAPTER 10
DESPERATE TIMES

Laura was beginning to get worried. Nikos had said he would be in Athens for a few days but it was now over a week since she'd heard from him. She obviously hoped nothing bad had happened to him, but she also wondered if perhaps their intimacy had spoilt their relationship. She had made all the moves and maybe he didn't like that. Mum had said always to be wary of Greek men.

Another day passed and then another. It was really crazy stupid that they'd never exchanged phone numbers, so she had no way of contacting him. She felt even more stupid when realising that she didn't even know where he lived. She'd never been to his house.

It was now ten days since she'd waved goodbye to him from the comfort of her bed after their night of lovemaking, and now came the doubts. Was it was her fault? Was it that she wasn't good enough? Who was she trying to kid? She knew she could never have lived up to his lavish lifestyle!

She couldn't face going to Corner Café to see Jeanie, not with all those people knowing (or thinking) he'd dumped her. Instead she walked into the village to buy some groceries. As she stood in the queue she was listening to the Greeks speaking. Her Greek wasn't that good but she heard the word 'catastrophe,' followed by the sight of them crossing themselves. Laura made the realisation that they were speaking about Nikos and his parents.

"Please!" Laura pleaded to the gathering. "Can you please tell me what you are saying - in English?"

A young mother holding on tightly to her wailing child told Laura, "There has been a terrible accident in Athens. Nikos has been critically injured, just as his parents were."

Hearing this devastating news, Laura nearly fainted. "Who can I speak to about this?" she begged.

"His yia-yia, sorry, his grandmother is in the café next door, but her English is not good," the crying baby's mother confirmed.

Laura left her purchases and ran to the café next door. "Please, who is the grandmother of Nikos?" she demanded frantically. The café owner pointed to a lady in black with her head in her hands. She was currently rocking back and forth in her chair.

"Can someone please explain to her that I am a friend of Nikos and I need to know what has happened to him?" she pleaded.

The café owner went over and put his hand on the lady's shoulder. He spoke gently to her and she looked at Laura and then gestured to her to come to her. "I know who you are, child. You have made my grandson very happy, but now he has gone. He has gone to join his parents," the old lady told a by now hysterical Laura.

"Oh my god!" she cried, almost passing out and falling to her knees. "When, what happened," she questioned, clamouring for more information.

"It was a car accident in Athens," the café owner explained. "He was very badly hurt and is in a coma. But they do not think he will make it."

"He IS still alive then?" she asked.

"Barely," the owner replied.

"Tell me how I can get to him," Laura asked. "I must go to him. He cannot be alone. I will get the next available flight."

The café owner was so helpful, having translated everything that she and the grandma had said, but now became a hero when he said he would take her to the airport when she was ready. He would find out all the details from someone who worked for the boat company.

Laura rushed home and threw a few clothes into a cabin bag and was ready when the café owner came to collect her.

He told her that the company had organised a car to pick her up at the airport in Athens and take her to the hospital.

Two hours later she was being driven through the busy streets of the capital city. The driver of the car worked for the company and told her, "I am there to help in any way I can." He told her that the entire workforce back on Kos was really upset about the accident.

Arriving at the hospital, it was obvious they were expecting Laura as she was immediately escorted up a flight of stairs and along a long corridor. As they reached the door at the end, it was opened by a gowned nurse.

"Are you Laura?" she asked.

"Yes," Laura confirmed. "But how do you know my name?"

"Before he became unconscious, Nikos was calling your name," the nurse smiled, trying to reassure her as much as possible. "Now don't be shocked by what you see. We are doing everything we can to make him comfortable. He's attached to a machine which is helping him to breathe, so you will see lots of tubes and wires connected to his body."

"Is he going to be okay?" Laura asked, thinking it was the most important question.

"Nobody can tell yet," the nurse replied with total honesty. "It depends on a great many things. There will be someone in the room to monitor him at all times, but you are welcome to stay as long as you like."

"Thank you," Laura said softly, as the emotions building up inside her began to take control.

"You could try talking to him," the nurse advised. "Hearing is one of the last senses to close down when er,"

"Don't say that," Laura snapped. "He is NOT going to die!"

"Anyway, you can go in now," the nurse advised her.

Laura took a deep breath, opened the door and stepped inside. Bright lights illuminated the room surrounding a medical bed positioned in the centre of it, with all sorts of bizarre machinery attached to Nikos making bleeping noises.

She summoned up the courage to look at her beloved Nikos as his body lay on the bed. His arm was in plaster and his leg was covered by a large frame. He was attached to the machinery by various wires and tubes, which were horrendous for Laura to see. She took a chair, placed it next to the bed and held his hand, squeezing it tightly.

"Oh, Nikos, how did we get here? What happened?" she asked, knowing there would be no answer. However, she still persevered with the questioning. "I was waiting for you but you didn't come. I thought you didn't want to see me anymore, but all this time I was worrying, you were lying here. I wish you could tell me how this happened and what it has done to your beautiful body."

She knew he couldn't answer, but these were some of the questions she needed to be answered. Her main question however was how many injuries he had and how they would affect him in the future. This was a question that no one could give an answer to at the moment.

The nurse at the back of the room keeping Laura company shifted her position. She was watching all the monitors intensely, a hard and laborious task. She smiled sympathetically at Laura, who in turn acknowledged her. This nurse could not speak English, but she could tell by the tone of Laura's voice that she was upset and worried about Nikos.

Laura continued to talk to Nikos, telling him how much she had missed him. She told him how she'd only been to the beach one time since he'd left for Athens. She hadn't even seen Jeanie for their usual coffees together as she really hadn't been in the mood.

She talked about the weather, the temperature of the sea, how many tourists there had been in the village, and how she'd spoken to the locals there and learnt of his accident.

She'd been sitting there talking to him for over two hours. From time to time, her voice waivered as emotion got the better of her but she carried on, as the nurse had told her Nikos might be able to hear what she was saying, even though he didn't stir at all.

The door opened and the consultant entered the room. Looking at the statistics gathered by the nurse, Laura watched as he shook his head. The doctor spoke quietly to the nurse, who almost whispered back to him. Laura's heart skipped a beat as he turned to face her.

"Hello my dear," he spoke to her in perfect English. "I believe you are the girlfriend of Nikos. I don't know how much you know about the accident."

"Nothing at all" croaked Laura.

"Well let me enlighten you," he began. "I'm sure you have many questions to ask me. I will try and tell you everything I know about his injuries."

"Thank you," Laura heard herself saying, but not really knowing why.

"He was on his way to a meeting at his office when a car mounted the pavement and struck him from behind. He was thrown several metres through the air, straight into a brick wall." The doctor stopped for a few seconds and looked at Laura, trying to gauge if she was taking all this in.

"He was conscious at first, but then he started drifting in and out consciousness," the doctor continued. "He was brought directly here to this trauma centre. Each time he came round, even if it was only for a few seconds he called out for you. We sedated him so we could assess his injuries and carry out various tests and procedures to help him."

"So how is he, Doctor?" Laura asked, craving the information.

"He has a few cracked ribs and his leg is badly damaged below the knee. We are not sure yet whether we will be able to save it or not."

"Oh no," Laura gasped; now feeling feint.

90

"We have stabilized the leg for the time being," the doctor continued. "However, our main concern at the moment is the injury to his head. The blow he received when hitting the wall could cause the brain to swell, and as it's contained in the hard shell of the skull it can cause pressure. This is what we are monitoring very closely."

"Is Nikos going to be okay?" Laura asked with moistening eyes.

"We may have to operate to relieve the pressure," the doctor instructed. "We cannot assess what damage there may be until the swelling reduces. There, now you know as much as we do," he concluded, giving her a slight smile in an attempt to make her feel less worried.

Obviously the smile did not work, as Laura looked at him and asked the question, "Will he live?"

"Well my dear girl that is the big question. Until we know if there is substantial damage to the brain or not, and if so, what areas of his body are functioning, we cannot really say. Meanwhile we are doing everything we can to save him and we are keeping him as comfortable as possible."

Laura bit her lip to stop herself screaming. She then composed herself enough to say," Thank you Doctor, thank you for your honesty. Can I stay?"

"For as long as you like," the doctor returned. "We may have to ask you to leave from time to time whilst we carry out necessary examinations. There is a room adjoining this one which is available for relatives to stay overnight, so they can be near their loved ones."

"Thank you so much," she managed to say.

"You're welcome my dear," the doctor replied. "You can hold his hand if you wish. I will keep you updated on everything."

Later when the nurses changed shifts and they checked the drips and monitors, Laura decided to take a quick shower. She hadn't left Nikos's side all day and now most of the night. Now dressed in clean clothes, she was about to return to sit with Nikos when a tremendous loud beeping sound came from his room. Laura was asked to wait in the adjoining room.

"What's happening?" she shouted hysterically.

"Please, let us look after him," the nurse demanded, not so politely now!

Laura returned to the private room provided, closed the door and sat on the bed. There was a lot of noise coming from the room, raised voices and banging sounds, but then it all went quiet. She waited for a moment, but the silence was deafening and she could wait no more!

She slowly opened the door to see what was going on, but the room was now empty. All the wires and lines were now hanging from the side of the machines, having all been disconnected. Laura feared the worst. Had Nikos passed, his body taken away without her being able to say goodbye?

She sat on the chair which had been next to his bed and just stared at the empty space where it had been; regretting the fact that she hadn't told him how much she loved him when she'd had the chance. All that time when they'd talked, they'd spoken about nothing important, just idle chit chat. Not once had she said, 'I love you.'

The door opened. It was the same doctor who she'd spoken to yesterday. His face looked grim.

"How is he?" Laura asked, desperate now for information.

"Not good," the doctor admitted.

"Please can I see him?" Laura begged the question.

"Not at the moment," he replied. "He's just on his way back from the theatre. We had to operate to release the pressure on his brain as it was causing him to fit. We hope we've managed to prevent any further damage, but again we will have to wait and see. Now please, Miss, go and get some rest now. We'll bring him back here when he's stabile."

"At least he's not dead," Laura remarked with a hint of relief.

"No. He must have been born under a lucky star. He is definitely a fighter. Let's just hope his luck stays with him. Now go now get some rest," the doctor repeated, hoping Laura would take notice this time. "If everything is okay, he will be here when you wake and you can continue your vigil." The doctor smiled in her direction as he wished her a goodnight, before leaving the once again empty room.

Laura was sure that she would never be able to sleep. Her mind was working overtime but she wanted to be here when they brought him back, however, her body took over. With it needing rest and recovery, she finally lost the battle and fell into a deep slumber. She dozed fitfully until she heard the door from the next room open. The nurse had come to prepare the room for the return of Nikos.

"Do you have any news?" Laura asked. The nurse didn't understand, so shrugged her shoulders and continued with her work.

Laura looked at the clock, amazed to see it was seven in the morning. She'd been sleeping for hours! Surely Nikos should have been brought back by now. There was no one to ask, she could see nobody around anywhere.

Another hour passed and Laura was by now frantic with worry! Finally, the door opened and they brought Nikos back, pushing him into the room in the same bed he'd been in yesterday and reconnecting him up to the monitors and machines as before.

"What happened?" Laura asked the nurse, when seeing his heavily bandaged head.

"He had another bleed, so we had to go in again to stem it," the nurse stated in broken English. "The swelling is going down now, so now we must wait."

Laura sat beside the bed. This time when she spoke to Nikos, she told him how much she loved him, how he'd turned her world upside down and how he'd taught her how love really should be.

Suddenly a loud bleeping sound came again from the machines. Nikos seemed to be choking and she was asked to leave whilst they tended to him. After what seemed an eternity, she was told she could go back inside the room.

Nikos no longer had the ventilator attached to him and he was lying perfectly still. She looked at him intently. His chest was rising and falling and happily Laura saw he was breathing for himself.

"We have removed the ventilator as he was fighting against it," Laura was told. "As you can see, he is breathing for himself, which is good news. However, we still have a long way to go. Come and sit with him. It's up to him now. When he's ready, he may regain consciousness. In the meantime, please keep talking to him. We know from past experience that it helps."

"Thank you all so very much," Laura said to the medical staff, all the time never taking her eyes off the patient.

For the rest of the day Nikos remained still, just breathing shallowly. Laura was exhausted and she felt her eyes closing. Falling asleep she relaxed her grip on his hand, but as she did so she felt a little squeeze on her fingers but had she imagined it? Looking at Nikos now, he looked and remained quite still.

She looked at the nurse who came across from the nurses' station to check the drips and monitor leads. She smiled at Laura, but without speaking, she went back to her station.

Laura's eyes began to close again as she was so tired. Trying hard to keep awake she shifted in her chair and looked lovingly at Nikos. At that very moment he opened his eyes, if only for a brief moment.

"Nurse - He's awake!" Laura shouted to the nurse, who came running to see what the fuss and commotion was about.

Slowly Nikos opened his eyes and screwed his face up, as if trying to focus. "Laura, is that you?" he asked with a confused expression.

"Yes, it's me Darling. It's me, Laura, I'm here," she confirmed.

Nikos closed his eyes again. The nurse contacted the doctor and he arrived to check things over.

"It would seem Nikos wants to join us," the doctor smiled. "We will reduce the sedation and see what happens."

A few hours later, Nikos stirred. Laura reacted immediately. "Nikos, come back to me," she pleaded.

He looked drunk but opened his eyes, managing to keep them open for a few seconds. "You really are here," he managed to say before closing his eyes again.

The medical staff needed to change his dressings so asked Laura to step outside for about half an hour. She went for a walk down the corridor to use her phone. Phoning her mother, she told her all that had happened. As she ended the conversation her phone instantly began to ring. She didn't recognise the number but answered it anyway.

"At last, I've got through to you. Thank goodness," it was Jeanie. "How's Nikos? How are you? Tell me everything."

"Hey slow down," Laura reacted.

"We have been so worried about you both. No one could tell us anything," Jeanie claimed, so Laura explained as much as she could.

"The village grapevine is saying the family is cursed! First the parents and now the son," Jeanie told Laura.

"That's awful," Laura replied. "Listen, I must go back and sit with Nikos now. Thank you for your concern. I will pass your good wishes onto Nikos and will ring you later."

As Laura returned to the room Nikos remained still, but as she approached his bed he opened his eyes and smiled.

"I'm a bit woozy, but I am so glad you are here," he muttered.

"I'm so glad you're here too, and still with us," she said, bending down and kissing him on the cheek. As she did she accidentally touched his ribs, making him wince with pain.

"OUCH!" he cried.

"Sorry," she said apologetically. "I forgot about your injuries for a moment."

"How can you forget them? I have a bandaged head and my leg is covered by a cage!"

"Oh, Nikos, I thought I'd lost you," Laura sighed.

The nurse persuaded Laura that she should go and get some sleep, reminding her that "Nikos also needs to rest." Reluctantly she agreed, returning to her little side room to rest.

She returned to his bedside a little later and was there when the consultant arrived to speak to Nikos. He told them both that it was good news about the head injury, saying it was just the scar that needed to heal. He was, however, very worried about the leg, which was giving him great cause for concern. Time alone would tell if the work done on the leg was successful. They would need to do further tests to determine this.

Nikos was told he might still need further surgery. Sadly, there was still the uncertainty as to whether he would need to have part of his leg amputated! Laura and Nikos both prayed this would not happen, but they would soon receive some devastating news.

Tests were carried out by injecting dye into the femoral artery to check the blood flow and nerve activity. Nikos had been waiting expectantly for the results of these tests and finally today would be the day when the results were revealed. The consultant entered the room and Nikos tried to work out from his facial expression what the news might be.

"It's not good news," the consultant said to Nikos." We've done all the tests and reviewed the results. I'm sorry to say, Nikos, we consider the best course of action is to perform a lower leg amputation. We will amputate the leg around two or three inches below the knee so that a prosthetic leg can be fitted and you will be able to walk unaided in the future."

"Why do you need to take the leg so high up, Doctor?" Nikos questioned.

"It's so we can use the skin and the muscle to form a cushion for you to walk on," Doctor Stavros informed him. Nikos still looked confused, so the doctor explained further. "What the surgeon will do is keep most of the skin and muscle and remove only the bone. The skin and muscle will then be neatly rolled into a cushion and stitched into place. The proteases will then be attached to a silicone leg liner fitted over the stump, with the excess skin and muscle acting as cushioning to make it more comfortable to walk on."

Nikos looked deep in thought, trying to take all this in. It was not what he wanted to hear. He really couldn't describe how he felt and all sorts of thoughts and questions were rampaging through his head. Would he be able to cope? Would he be able to walk unaided? What would this leg look like? Would he be embarrassed to go swimming, do any sports or even wear shorts? In fact would he even be able to go swimming in the protease? Would he still be able to ride his beloved motorbike?

'Oh my God what about Laura,' he thought, as the seriousness of the situation he now found himself in suddenly hit home. He thought about the future with Laura and wondered if she would be able to accept him as an amputee. Would she ever want to make love with him again?

Nikos was usually a positive thinking guy and looked for the best in the worst of situations, but at this moment, he couldn't find anything positive about all this. It seemed there was no alternative but to lose part of his leg, and it needed to be done sooner rather than later. They had tried so hard to save his leg but, sadly, it was not to be.

Nikos sat motionless and deep in thought. His beloved Laura would be back soon and he would have to tell her about this dilemma. Putting his own reactions aside, he thought how it might affect her. She'd seen him with the visible injuries to his face, along with the surgery scars on his head and even his shaven head. His leg had always been covered with the cage that had been stabilising it when she was there. He himself had been revolted by the damage to his leg and if he were honest, it would not have surprised him if they'd said previously that they couldn't save it.

Doctor Stavros popped back into the room. "We can schedule the operation for the day after tomorrow," he announced." Are you okay with that? Once done, after a few days for you to rest, followed by a week or two for the stump to heal, we can start to think about your rehabilitation and have you walking."

When he left, Nikos sat with his head in his hands. How had it all come to this? Surely he'd had his fair share of tragedy in his life with losing his parents as such a young age. Just when life was beginning to feel good, fate dealt him another blow. He wondered to himself if it might have been better had he not survived the accident and died that day. Just then the door opened and in walked Laura.

"How's my wounded soldier today then? Are you ready to come home?" He looked up at her and she could tell by his expression that something was seriously wrong and really troubling him. She could now see he had tears in his eyes and felt a strange sensation course through her. All through this terrible ordeal she had never before seen Nikos cry.

"What's wrong?" she gushed, rushing to his side to offer comfort and support.

"Everything!" he answered, his face now wet from the tears.

"Tell me, Nikos, you can tell me anything," she said, tightly holding his hand.

"I won't be coming home for a little while, Laura, and then in fact, a lot less of me will be coming home!" Laura looked confused.

"I don't understand, Nikos," she said.

Nikos took a deep breath and delivered the news he'd never wanted to hear, telling her about the amputation. "The doctor says we have no choice, it has to be done," he told an awestruck Laura.

"Oh, Nikos, my love, I don't know what to say," she sympathised.

"There isn't anything to say," Nikos replied. He then told her all about the procedure, as he'd been told himself only a few moments earlier.

"And will you be able to walk afterwards?" she asked.

"Yes I will," Nikos said defiantly. "Laura, if the famous world war two pilot Douglas Bader could learn to walk again and fly his plane on two tin legs, I'm sure it will be able to do it on one! And with today's advanced technology, I have a far better chance than he did way back then." Nikos was trying to make light of it, but inside his stomach was churning with every word spoken.

"What can I do to help?" Laura questioned lovingly.

"You can stay away until all this is over and done with. Let me deal with it in my own way," he told her, and this shocked her greatly.

"But Nikos, I want to be here with you and help you," she pleaded.

"But you can't help me with this, Laura. I need to do this all by myself." He looked her straight in the eye as he said forcefully, "Laura, please go home, get on with your own life and leave me in peace!"

Laura looked downtrodden. Obviously, he felt she was of no use to him at all. Holding back her emotions, she stood strong and replied, "Okay I will go back to Kefalos, but when you are ready to return, I will be waiting for you. I'll be waiting for you whether you like it or not! You cannot get rid of me that easily, Nikos. I do not walk away when someone I love needs a shoulder to cry on."

"And as I don't have a leg to stand on, well only one leg, I might need someone to lean on for a while when this is over," Nikos said, trying to muster a smile.

"Nikos, I will be there when you want or need me, it's up to you. I will go now, but I hope you will be in touch soon." Laura said, holding back the tears.

She closed the door and walked down the corridor, shocked and stunned that Nikos had told her to go away. Was she so useless that she couldn't comfort or help him. But of course, she could not imagine what poor Nikos must be going through. She phoned her mother.

"Can you collect me from the airport tonight?" she asked Jenny. "I will be alone, as I'm coming home without Nikos."

The staff at the centre had been fantastic and he was already working out how he could thank them for their care and compassion. Perhaps he could fund another trauma unit like this one that his family had previously paid for.

The doctors, nurses and physiotherapists' all marvelled at his determination. Even when he was totally frustrated because things were not going right he was always positive, polite and grateful. They all considered him to be a model patient, always eager to do more by setting himself goals and timeframes, and always verbalising his commitment by saying, "I can do this - I WILL do this - Come on Nikos – Do it!"

It had been a terrible time and a truly horrible ordeal for Nikos. Many times, over the past couple of months he'd wished he hadn't sent Laura away. Many times he wished she'd been there with him by his side, but he'd been foolish and thought he could handle it alone – Boy was he wrong!

First to come was the surgery. He'd been wheeled into the operating theatre and given an epidural. After only seconds his legs turned to concrete. He could not even move a toe!

He was awake all through the opp, although a sheet was put between his eyes and his legs so he couldn't actually see anything. This meant that, although he could not see the surgeon taking his leg, he could hear the swish-swish-swish of the medical saw as he took away the bone.

For the next fifteen minutes he could smell something like meat being cooked on the barbeque, a not too unpleasant smell until he realised it was his own flesh being cooked! It was in fact the surgeon fusing the nerve ends in the stump before stitching it all back together.

After the opp was completed in around forty-five minutes, he was taken to the recovery room to wait for the feeling to return to his leg (and stump) before taking him back to his room. This was so they could monitor him in case anything went wrong. Four hours later he was wheeled back to his own room, and this was when he really wished he hadn't sent her away and Laura was there waiting for him.

The next two hours were spent just looking at the ceiling. He felt numb, as though all this was happening to somebody else! All of a sudden, the last remnants of anaesthetic left his body and – WHOOSH – he felt something like a cold wind rush through his veins and the pain began!

For the next three days he could not move his stump. Every time he moved even only an inch, it felt like being stabbed with a razor sharp samurai sword! Morphine became his best friend!

On the fourth day after the operation, thankfully he woke and the pain was gone. After breakfast, he was forced to leave his bed and sit in an armchair, although he couldn't see the point of it. It was hard on his ass and nowhere near as comfy as the bed.

Later, when the doctor came to check on him, Nikos asked if he could be provided with a wheelchair so he could go and explore his new home.

"Certainly Nikos," the doctor smiled. "And if you're ready for a wheelchair, perhaps you are ready to wheel yourself down to the gymnasium and begin your rehabilitation?"

Later that day a male nurse came with a chair. "Here you are," he smiled. "Here are your new wheels."

He helped Nikos move from the chair to the wheelchair. Nikos thanked him for the help – this time, but said that this would be the last time he'd accept this kind of help, as he had to do this for himself.

Nikos put his hands on the rims of the wheels and pushed. Oh my lord – This was the hardest thing he'd ever done before in his life! This wheelchair was the best piece of exercise equipment he'd ever used. He could feel himself getting fitter and stronger with every revolution, as he slowly moved along the corridor!

Although it was hard going for him, it lifted his spirits and gave him the confidence to believe his life was NOT over. Yes it would be different from now on, but on this very day his new life had begun!

CHAPTER 11
REHABILITATION

"Hello Nikos," - "Good morning Nikos," – "How are you today, Nikos?" all the ladies in the gym greeted him every morning. One by one, they were all slightly falling a little in love with this very good looking Greek man, although what they were falling in love with most was his attitude towards his rehabilitation. It was obvious that he was a fighter, and he was not going to let a little thing like an amputated leg get in the way of the rest of his life.

It was now eight days since the operation. Nikos was consistently the first patient in the gym at nine in the morning, and was always the last to leave at half past twelve. He spent the first hour or so doing leg exercises. He lay on an exercise bed and his personal physio placed a two kilo weight attached with Velcro to the bottom of his right ankle, and attached another to the stump of his left. The idea was that by lifting each leg alternatively fifty times each with a one minute break between reps, he would build up the thigh muscles and prepare them for the extra effort he would need to balance on his proteases, when it was made to measure for him.

Then it was time for the dreaded bars. Although Nikos couldn't understand what possible benefit it was to him, hopping along the twin bars on one leg, his physio explained that it was helping with his balance, whilst also building the strength in his arms which he would need for the first two or three months to help him use the crutches, to support his weight until walking with the proteases became more natural to him.

His physiotherapist was a lovely girl with the name of 'Callista,' which had the meaning – 'Most Beautiful.' And she was a very beautiful young girl, who, although only in her early twenties was extremely good at her chosen profession.

"Let me look at your stump, Nikos," Callista said on this particular visit. After studying it for a minute or two, she smiled at him and said, "Okay, I think we are ready."

"Hum – Ready for what?" Nikos questioned curiously.

"I think we are ready for your massage," Callista confirmed.

"That doesn't sound too bad," Nikos smiled. However, he was wrong!

Nikos lay on his front with his face on the bed and with his left leg stump raised in the air behind him. First Callista began by gently rubbing the amputated area. She then began softly tapping the skin with her fingertips, this was followed by more gentle and relaxing massaging. Nikos was enjoying this and was almost drifting off to sleep.

"Okay Nikos, are you ready?" she questioned again.

"Am I ready for what?" Nikos asked again.

"Are you ready for pain?" Callista smiled.

Before he could respond, the very beautiful physio began knocking seven bails out of his stump, slapping it as though playing the bongos' very loudly. Although painful, Nikos began laughing, and this made all the girls in the gym look in his direction. Very soon there was laughter everywhere.

Callista told Nikos the reason for this was to prepare his leg for the discomfort of wearing the proteases, explaining that whatever pain and discomfort it gave him would not be as bad as this. He understood the reasoning and in a strange way, looked forward to his 'daily' massage routine.

A few days later the specialist came to measure him for the proteases to be made. Sitting in his wheelchair so they could move him around more easily, they covered his stump with a silicone leg liner and then covered that with something resembling clingfilm, although it was far more advanced than the type you buy in the supermarket. His stump was then covered in a sickly warm runny plaster, which felt horrible when first applied, but even worse for Nikos as it started to go cold and turn rock hard. After thirty minutes, the two men working on the leg pulled it off and happily showed Nikos a perfect mould, which would be used to have the top of the proteases made, the piece which the silicone leg liner would attach to.

At last Nikos could see light at the end of the tunnel and this spurred him on even more to prepare himself for his departure back to the island of Kos and to Laura, the girl he loved. By now he thought constantly about her. She became his reason to get proficient at walking, and in the future be able to return to some kind or resemblance of his more, sporty past.

One morning whilst in the gym, Callista came to see him with some good news. "Nikos, the men are waiting in your room with your new proteases," she beamed. "They ask if you can go back and have a fitting."

He didn't even say goodbye to the girls in his excitement and left the gymnasium immediately. He'd been waiting for this moment for almost a month, and did not want to waste another second.

"Can you sit on the bed please Nikos?" the main man of the two asked. He did as requested.

They put the silicone leg liner on his leg and then took the proteases from a box. Nikos looked at it and the men saw he was not happy.

"Don't worry Nikos," the main man instructed, "it's not finished yet. Once we are happy with the fit we will fit it with the fake skin, and then it will look much like a normal leg," hearing this made Nikos smile.

As they attached the leg to the liner, Nikos heard the reassuring click-click-click as the two married together. The two men grabbed hold of an arm each and lifted Nikos to a standing position.

"Try and balance when we let go of you," the main man said. As they did so, Nikos cried out in anguish.

105

"It's no good," he shouted. "It's no good at all!"

Just as he shouted this, Callista entered the room. "What are you moaning about? Come on Nikos, try and balance like you do in the rehabilitation."

But it's no good, Callista," he said again. "Can't you see – it's too bloody long!"

"What do you mean?" the beautiful physio questioned.

"Look at it," he demanded. "The fake leg is an inch longer than my real one! How am I supposed to balance and stand straight?" Upon hearing this, Callista and the two men burst out laughing, making Nikos even angrier until hearing the explanation.

"That's why we haven't fitted the fake skin to it yet," the main man said, taking out and waving an adjustable spanner at Nikos. "When we leave here today, it will be a perfect fit. Then we will take it back to our workshop and put the skin on."

"How long will that take?" Nikos asked feeling a little deflated, like a child felt an hour after opening the presents on Christmas day.

"Not long," said the man. Then noticing his sadness he told Nikos, "I will return with it this afternoon. I promise." Instantly the smile returned to Nikos's face.

Now he had his proteases, he quickly learned to attach it, remove it, and walk on it, although he had to admit that it was a lot more difficult than he thought it would be.

In the gym, Callista encouraged him to walk around the bars one handed, instead of walking through the bars with two. After a couple of days he had the confidence to let go of the bar completely, but could only manage two steps before grabbing the bar again. Callista could see he was frustrated by this and put her arm around his shoulder to offer her support.

Day by day he became more and more expert at walking on his new mode of transport, and within two weeks, with a resounding round of applause he managed to walk twenty yards unaided, at least he did on the rubberised floor of the gymnasium.

"I want to walk in the garden," he announced to Callista.

"Come on then," she beamed and grabbed his crutches.

"I don't want them" he demanded, pointing at the offending articles.

"Okay Nikos, but I'll bring them just in case," Callista confirmed. Ten minutes later they returned. Nikos had successfully achieved his 'maiden voyage and felt triumphant! He couldn't wait to tell Laura all about it.

The time Nikos had spent in hospital was certainly no picnic for Laura. Each day she tried to busy herself with gardening, decorating around the house and taking long walks around Kefalos. Now when she went swimming, she felt lonely. Before this had happened she'd enjoyed the solitude, but she now missed Nikos so much.

She met Jeanie in 'Bravo' a few times, but her mind was always elsewhere. Jeanie understood and she felt for her friend. She knew how much Nikos had come to mean to Laura. Since their first meeting they'd been inseparable, but it was now hard to know if this relationship would survive.

Laura had been heartbroken at the decision made by Nikos to send her away in what she thought was his hour of need, and because of this, her self-esteem had again plummeted She thought that Nikos obviously felt (wrongly) that his initial recovery was of no concern to her.

Jeanie was worried about Laura, but apart from being there for her she could do very little to help.

At last, eight long weeks after she'd left him at the hospital in Athens, Nikos phoned her. Her relief was instant. He'd phoned to say he was coming home to Kefalos in a few days and wondered if she might come to his house to be with him during his rehabilitation. Although leaving Athens, he was given strict instructions that it was a condition of his release that he attended a local clinic in Kos to continue with his recovery. The fact he was coming home made Laura very happy. The fact that he was asking for her help made her feel ecstatic!

"One problem though, Nikos," she said during their phone conversation. "I don't know where your house is, and have no idea of the address or how to get there."

"Don't worry," Nikos laughed, "I'll send a driver to collect you from your home and take you there."

Two days later his driver collected Nikos from the airport. On the way to his home they stopped to collect a very surprised, happy and excited Laura.

"Nikos," she cried, melting into his arms.

"Careful," he cried. "You'll knock me over!"

"Sorry," she said apologetically.

"Only joking," Nikos replied. "Please don't let the crutches put you off, Laura. I promise to lose them as quickly as possible."

"They don't bother me, Nikos," she assured him. "I am just so happy that you are finally here with me again."

"Please take us home, Christos," Nikos said politely to the driver, who duly obliged.

Several large houses had been built high on the hill above Kefalos, each with enormous areas of land around them. Nikos's home stood quite a distance away from the other properties.

The wall around the extensive garden was covered with a blue flowered vine, which added extra privacy. Large electric wrought iron gates provided the entrance and they swung open as the car transporting Laura and the returning Nikos was driven through and up the gravel driveway, surrounded on both sides by flower beds, rockeries, water features and statues.

A multi arched porch sheltered the front entrance to the villa, before which the driveway divided in front at the house, one way led to the garage and the other to the rear garden area, housing the pool, gazebo, sun terraces and outdoor barbecue. It had all been meticulously planned to catch the sun during the day, with shady areas for eating and relaxation when the sun was too hot.

But if the outside of the house was impressive, the inside was spectacular, boasting six bedrooms, all with ensuite bathrooms, a fully equipped gymnasium, and to one side of the gym there was a sauna.

Although Nikos had told her quite a lot about his life, she now came to realise there was still a lot to learn about his opulent lifestyle.

As they approached, the front door was opened. This was followed by the sound of frantic barking, as three large black and white English setters came bounding up to greet them. Laura had been brought up with dogs so she was happy to be greeted by these lovely creatures. Walking slowly but purposely in their wake was an ageing red setter, although not as energetic as the others, his wagging tail showed how pleased he was to see them, and was particularly happy to see that his master was home.

Laura took a closer look around at the reception area and couldn't believe what she was seeing. It was like stepping into a movie set.

With the help of Christos, Nikos was seated on a chair in the lounge. Next to his luxurious armchair stood a walking frame to help him get around indoors, whilst parked at the back of the room was a top of the range motorised wheelchair, which had been ordered in advance of his return. This would make it easier for him to go around the garden, until fully mastering the proteases.

On the table next to Nikos were various boxes of differing medications, his favourite being the 'morphine lollipops' given to him specially by Doctor Stavros, who told him to suck them slowly should he suffer any pain.

Alone at last, Laura rushed to him. His smile said it all. He held out his arms and she fell into them. They hugged for what seemed like an eternity with neither speaking, no words needed.

Laura sat on the floor next to him with her hand on the arm of his chair. Both were apprehensive about what would happen next.

"Do you remember where we left off before I went to Athens?" Nikos asked, taking a hold of her hand. "I know it was a lifetime ago, but I seem to remember we made love."

"Yes, we did" Laura blushed, "and it was wonderful," she said, remembering how sweet and gentle Nikos had been, and the total ecstasy she'd experienced for the first time in her life.

"The memory of that kept me going these past weeks," Nikos whispered. "Maybe we should refresh that memory?"

"I'd love to". Laura replied, with a tingling excitement rushing over her.

His heart was beating fast as he stood and walked purposefully towards the steps. He held out his hand to Laura. "Would you help me a little please?"

"Do you need me to help you with the stairs?" she questioned.

"No, but I need you," he smiled. "I need you to come with me."

He manoeuvred himself up the stairs quite skilfully, just as he'd been taught by Callista in Athens. Laura was so proud of him. Again, he held out his hand to her.

"Come," he said. "I want to show you something."

Laura's heart skipped a beat and Nikos held his breath. Could they both handle this? He took Laura into one of the bedrooms. The curtains were drawn and there were small lights in the alcove above the bed. In the semi darkness they lay on the bed and slowly undressed each other. When Laura caught sight of the prosthetic leg, she inhaled deeply.

"Are you okay?" Nikos asked.

"I'm more than okay, Nikos," Laura replied.

"Are you afraid to see my leg?" he asked.

"No Nikos, I'm not afraid because it's part of you," she smiled. "And being part of you, I think it's beautiful."

He slid under the covers and removed the prosthetic. He turned to Laura and kissed her. Their bodies entwined. No thought was given to anything but their lovemaking.

After, when both satisfied, they lay together just long enough to get their breath back and then, again they began the ritual of stroking each other's bodies, exploring every inch of each other until both were ready yet again.

"We can shower together if you like," said Nikos.

"Of course," Laura replied.

Nikos used a crutch to help him into the bathroom. Whilst he'd been away at the hospital it had been arranged for builders to come to the house and convert his bathroom into a wet room, with grab bars on each wall and a special seat for him to sit on whilst taking a shower.

Laura was amazed. What a fabulous room they'd built for him. The shower was about three times the size of hers at home, room enough for him to enter in his wheelchair after removing his leg, positioning himself on the seat and then moving the chair to the side whilst showering. This time however, he had Laura to lovingly remove his leg for him.

They enjoyed soaping each other and it was inevitable that, yet again they were going to make love. Sex had never been so enjoyable. She'd never felt this way with Martin. She knew that this was real love.

CHAPTER 12
AN IMPORTANT QUESTION

They'd returned to the restaurant where they had their first romantic date and had later that evening made love for the first time. It had become one of their favourite restaurants.

This evening, Nikos wore a crisp white shirt and black trousers, whilst Laura wore a full-length midnight blue, off the shoulder dress. The dress was accompanied by a blue stoned necklace which Nikos had bought for her. She suspected the stones were sapphires and diamonds, but never asked. Anyway it didn't matter what they were, because she loved it.

Laura was seated by the waiter who then disappeared to fetch two menus, whilst Nikos was helped from his crutches to be seated in a chair facing her. As he studied the menu, Laura thought Nikos looked a bit off tonight, maybe even a little nervous. She thought he could be tentative about being seen out in public, with everyone knowing about his accident and the fact he now wore a false leg.

The meal was eaten mainly in silence, after which the waiter brought coffee and brandy for the pair. Laura could take his uneasiness no longer and felt she needed to break the silence and discover the problem.

"Is everything okay, Nikos?" she questioned.

He put his hand across the table and took hold of hers. He then looked directly into her eyes and smiled. "I need to ask you something," he revealed.

"Anything wrong?" she returned. Again Nikos smiled at her naivety.

"Laura," he hesitatingly began. "All of my life I have dreamed of finding the right girl to spend the rest of my life with, and now I believe that with you, I have. I want to spend the rest of my life living with you and starting a family with you." By now everyone in the restaurant had stopped what they were doing and were all staring in their direction as Nikos continued.

"My darling Laura, would you do the honour of becoming my wife? Laura, will you please marry me?" Laura's eyes filled with tears, but her answer stunned him!

"Nikos my darling, you are a wonderful person and I love you so much, but I cannot marry you," she replied in tears.

Before she had a chance to explain her decision, Nikos, to the best of his abilities, walked out of the restaurant and staggered along the beach road as fast as his crutches would take him! Laura sat abandoned at the table. She'd wanted to explain why she could not marry him, but he'd left without giving her the chance.

Sadly she made her own way home. It seemed a long weary trek, walking in high heels and evening dress with people staring at her as she passed the various tavernas and restaurants. However, she took little notice of them. She only wanted to get back to her home and really think about what had just happened.

She lay in bed that night thinking how much they had already been through in their lives. She loved Nikos and had never experienced real love before, but it was because she loved him that she couldn't marry him.

All that she'd really wanted had been thrown away by her in one sentence, when she'd told Nikos, "I'm sorry I can't marry you." Where did she go from here, and what did her future hold for her now, a life on her own? Possibly, but she didn't know. That night, feeling heartbroken, she cried herself to sleep.

The following morning she tried to ring Nikos on his mobile, but his phone was switched off. Perhaps he'd gone to the office in Kos town, or worse still, maybe he'd blocked her number. She tried ringing the office but no one picked up, so she tried the house number which Nikos had given her.

This time her call was accepted. It was Costas the gardener who answered.

"Is Nikos there? I need to speak to him," Laura pleaded.

"I'm sorry but he's not here," Costas answered.

"Are you sure, Costas, or has he told you to say that because he's ignoring me?" she queried.

"No Madam, I promise you. He left on the early plane to Athens this morning," Costas revealed.

"Why? Has he gone back to the hospital?" Laura queried.

"No Madam, he said he was going to Athens to look for an apartment to live there," Costas revealed. "I'm not sure when he will be back."

"Thank you Costas," she said, putting down the phone and ending the call.

She thought about what the gardener had said. Surely it couldn't be true. Costas must be mistaken. Nikos would never leave his beloved Kefalos for Athens. She tried his mobile number again but no answer. She desperately wanted to explain to him why she couldn't marry him, so wanting to explain the real reason for her rejection. She phoned several more times over the next few days, but Nikos never answered.

Laura began to feel that she was a complete failure at love and relationships, but knew she had to pull herself together. She'd gotten over one long term relationship with Martin and could get over another, but the trouble was, she didn't want to get over this one with Nikos. She wanted it more than anything she'd ever wanted, but she couldn't take Nikos's dream away. It had been what had kept him going after his parents were killed.

Laura knew that it was his big dream to have children, to produce an heir, male or female, but an heir to take over the company in his retirement. However, what Nikos didn't know was that Laura was sure she could never give him a child. All that time she'd spent trying to get pregnant with

Martin but without success, she could not put Nikos through that. Better that he find another girl to give him the family he craves.

She knew that she would be very happy being the wife of Nikos, especially with all the luxury which would go with it, but she could not bear the idea of making him unhappy. Yes, he would smile on the outside, but on the inside he would hurt. There would always be something missing.

After the rejection, Nikos walked carefully along the beach road to his newly acquired automatic car and drove back to the villa. He was angry! He'd planned his proposal meticulously and the time seemed right. They were getting on so well and shared many things. Laura had been his rock during his time in hospital, but perhaps all she had felt was sympathy for him. They'd had so much fun before the accident, but maybe she didn't feel the same way about him now he was disabled. He knew she was a loving and very caring person, but he wanted love real love from her and not sympathy.

He made a reservation to fly to Athens on the dawn flight from Kos. He packed a few clothes and left notes for Costas saying he had urgent business in Athens and had to find a place to stay long term, maybe to live in permanently.

He sat all night pondering what had happened, feeling sad and let down by the girl he loved. He felt angry that she'd misled him about her feelings, but most of all he felt a deep loss. He thought she'd been everything to him for a short time and all his prayers had been answered, but now that was all over!

Laura busied herself tending to the garden, decorating in the house and continuing to go for the long walks she usually enjoyed. But it was no longer like it had been. Every beach she visited, every cove she explored and every hill she climbed reminded her of the great times she'd shared with

Nikos. She tried so many times to shake him from her thoughts but found it impossible. She just could not do it.

She knew she would never lose those memories. She'd told her mother, Jenny that she and Nikos were having a little time apart as he was busy in Athens. Jenny could see the sadness in her daughter's eyes but felt she shouldn't question her further about it, thinking that if Laura wanted to share her problem with her, she would when she was ready to do so.

Laura met her good friend, Jeanie, and tried to explain what had happened to her. Although she was a shoulder to cry on, Jeanie couldn't understand why Laura was so insistent that she couldn't marry Nikos.

Days dragged and weeks passed at a snail's pace. Laura thought about returning to England and picking up her life where she'd left off. The boss at her work had said she would be welcomed back anytime. She loved Kefalos but was now finding it difficult without Nikos in her life.

Nikos had found an apartment in Athens and had agreed to rent with a view to buying, but he spent very little time there. He sometimes slept at the office and sometimes in a hotel, at least there was something going on there. When he was alone in the flat, all he could think about was Laura. Even after everything that had passed between them on that fateful night when his pride had been hurt, he still wanted her so much.

He decided he needed to know the reason for her rejection, as it was eating into him constantly. He couldn't concentrate on anything and his enthusiasm for work was waning. He stood and banged his fist on the table! He had to find out why she'd said 'No!'

Picking up the office phone he dialled Laura's number. It rang several times, but then he lost his nerve and disconnected the call. Laura didn't recognise the number of the call she'd just missed. She tried ringing it, but the message said the number could not be reached.

Nikos paced up and down in his office. His head hurt, his leg hurt, but more than anything his feelings and emotions were hurting. He picked up the phone again and rang Laura's number Laura saw it was the same number she'd missed previously, but as she didn't recognise it, she was a little hesitant to answer. However, eventually she did.

"Hello," she said curiously. She was surprised when a familiar voice said her name. "Nikos, is that you?" she questioned, beginning to shake with emotion

"Yes, it's me," he replied.

"Nikos, how are you?" she asked, but he didn't reply to this question.

"I need to speak to you," he told her. "Can we meet sometime tomorrow?" Laura wasn't sure what to say. Did she really want to see him, or did she not? Her head was jangled. "Please Laura, I need to see you," Nikos pleaded. Reluctantly she agreed. They made arrangements to meet the next day.

Nikos stood looking at the phone in his office, had he done the right thing contacting her? He convinced himself that he had, because he needed to know Laura's reasons. He left for the airport and took the afternoon flight to Kos. A couple of hours later he arrived back at the villa in Kefalos, ready for a sleepless night ahead.

The next morning he woke with anxiety about his meeting with Laura. It was as though all his nerve endings were trembling. He drove the Mercedes automatic to meet her where they'd arranged. Laura was waiting when he arrived. She walked slowly towards him but neither spoke, they just stood staring at each other.

"Why?" Nikos finally managed to ask. "Why won't you marry me? Do you no longer love me?"

"Nikos I love you very, very much," she admitted.

"Then why reject me?" he asked, wide eyed.

"Nikos, it's because I love you so much that I rejected you. When we first met you told me about your dream for the future, to marry and have children and to be able to share your success with them," she started with Nikos listening intently. "Nikos, I cannot give you children. I cannot make your dream come true, but more than that, I cannot take that dream away from you."

Nikos looked deep in thought for a few seconds, but then spoke. "It's true, Laura, that had been my dream, but now I realise that without you in my life that dream is pointless. My dream now is to marry you and spend my life with you. I know we can be happy together I'm sure, children or no children."

"But Nikos, I will always know that you changed your dream for me," she challenged.

"I changed my dream because of you," he replied. "I changed my dream because I love you, Laura. It was not a difficult decision. You ARE my dream."

"I don't know what to say," Laura said breaking a stunned silence.

"Please think about it, Laura," he appealed. "If you will meet me tonight at the restaurant around eight, you can give me your decision then."

He returned to his car and drove away, leaving Laura in a daze. Could she really believe he could change his dream about having children, or would he blame her in the future for not being able to provide him with a family?

As it grew dark, she readied herself to meet Nikos and give him her decision, which could be life changing. She arrived at the restaurant a little early. Sitting alone she gazed up at the sky and a million stars glistened back at her. Laura remembered how stars had always been important in her life. Her sister, Emily had always been referred to as a bright star.

"Look to the stars," Dad had said to her. "Look to the stars whenever you feel sad or alone and I will be there for you."

"What shall I do dad," she asked the brightest star in the night sky. "I cannot give him what he wants."

She looked up again and noticed that three of the brightest stars were now in a line above the horizon. Laura made her decision.

Nikos entered the restaurant and sat opposite her at the table. He stretched out his arms and offered her his hand. She took it. "Are you ready to tell me your decision?" he asked.

"Ask me again," she said, squeezing his hand. "Ask me the question.

"Laura my darling, please would you do me the honour of being my wife," he smiled. "Will you marry me?"

"I love you Nikos and I would love to be your wife," she replied.

"But?" he queried.

"But nothing," she replied. "Nikos – YES – I will marry you."

Nikos stood gingerly, turned Laura round and kissed her. He took a small box from his pocket it and gave it to her. By the light of the full moon the contents of the box sparkled. Laura saw the box held a ring with three perfect diamonds in a straight line. She took it from the box and looked at it, noticing that it matched the stars in the sky.

Although she couldn't see it, Nikos told her it was engraved on the inside with the words, 'When the stars align.'

He placed the ring on Laura's finger. Instantly they both knew they'd found true love and happiness together.

CHAPTER 13
WEDDING PLANS

Nikos had no close family as such, apart from his grandmother. However, because of his popularity he was the village's son. Everyone was happy to accept the open invitation to attend his marriage ceremony to Laura.

Being a traditionalist, Nikos had gone to see Laura's mother and Yiannis to ask their permission to marry Laura, and they certainly approved of her choice of husband. Laura asked Yiannis to give her away.

"Laura, I would be proud to walk you down the aisle," Yiannis told her. "I will be proud to give you away."

Nikos had insisted he paid for Laura's wedding dress, so Laura and her mother were flying to Athens for the day to look at the fantastic stores and hopefully find that very special dress for her. Her mother, Jenny also wanted to find an outfit that her daughter would be proud to see her in. They felt they had a lot to live up to since a lot of Nikos's more wealthy friends and clients were invited to the wedding, so they didn't want to look out of place in the middle of such wealthy, designer clothed celebrities.

Nikos had taken them to the airport to catch the early plane to Athens. Once boarded, it was a matter of forty-five minutes before they landed in Athens.

Although Nikos had told them to take a taxi from the airport into Athens City, Laura and Jenny decided to take the metro. It was quick and comfortable and put English subways to shame. All the stations along the line were built in marble and the carriages were impeccably clean, with announcements being made at the approach to each station.

Reaching the station nearest to the retail centre they disembarked, and after leaving the metro station they headed for a little coffee shop in the square. Here they had coffee and croissants to give them energy for the task ahead.

It was good for Laura to spend quality time with her mother like this. Jenny had been there for her when she'd first arrived in Kos, and had helped her come to terms with the end of her previously unhappy relationship. She was really pleased to see Laura happy now with Nikos, who she also liked very much. She joked that she liked him even more after discovering he was loaded! Yiannis had told Jenny that Nikos was from a good family and was a good man. He also told her that Nikos would take very good care of her daughter and that pleased her no end.

There were several high-class wedding gown retailers along the length of one of the streets, and this was where they headed next. Laura had been told by her friend Jeanie which was the best.

"Otherwise you could go in each one and find the same designer dresses over and over again at vastly differing prices," Jeanie had revealed. Laura laughed at this.

Looking around, Laura would never have dreamed she would ever be shopping in such expensive shops yet here she was, with no financial limitations looking for the wedding dress of her dreams. She was a little nervous going into the shop as her knowledge of the Greek language was limited, but having her mum there with her, who by now was almost fluent in the language, helped calm her nerves. She really wasn't sure what she wanted, but had thought of something plain, but classic. She explained to the consultant what she was looking for and several dresses were brought for her to look at.

A white satin dress caught her eye as she went through the samples and Laura asked to view it properly. She thought this was the one and loved it. When she returned from the changing room wearing the dress, Jenny also loved it.

"You look like a fairytale princess," Jenny told her daughter proudly. "But I think it needs a veil."

121

Laura agreed with Mum and began looking on the rack for that one veil which would match the dress perfectly.

"Why are you laughing?" Jenny questioned, as her daughter began to laugh.

"Mum, look," Laura returned. "Look at that tiara. It has three diamante stars in a row, just like my engagement ring."

"It must be a sign," Jenny said. "The stars are perfectly aligned. I think you should have it."

After shopping most of the day buying a dress for Jenny, which Laura said made her look like a movie star, and Laura had shopped alone for sexy underwear for the wedding night, as jenny thought this was too personal for her to help with, they then bought matching outfits for the bridesmaids.

Now really tired from a good days shopping, heavily laden with parcels and with aching feet from all the walking, they hailed a taxi and returned to the airport and from there they caught the evening plane back to Kos. When they landed, Nikos was waiting to collect them and return them to Kefalos. He opened the boot of the car and filled it with her parcels.

"Did you manage to get everything?" he asked.

"Almost," Laura replied.

Nikos dropped them off at their respective houses and Laura showered and went directly to bed. It had been a long tiring day, but overall an enjoyable one. The main thing was that she was content with her purchases.

The wedding was becoming a reality now. Nikos and Laura were both excited and nervous about it in equal measures. Her sister Suzie's daughters, Maisie and Mia, were to be bridesmaids, with Suzie being Matron of Honour. Laura's friend, Jeanie, who was responsible for Laura meeting Nikos, was Chief Bridesmaid, a role she was very proud to perform.

Everything was manic in the weeks leading up to the wedding, booking flights and organising accommodation for invited family and friends who'd accepted the invitation. This all took an amazing amount of planning and by the time they'd finished, both Laura and Nikos were absolutely frazzled!

"I think we deserve a day off to relax," Nikos said, and Laura agreed. "Why don't you phone your mother and Yiannis and see if they'd fancy a trip to Nisyros for the day?" Nikos suggested. "I haven't been out on the yacht for ages."

When questioned, Jenny and Yiannis were delighted at the prospect of going out on the yacht. They said they could be ready in an hour and agreed to meet at the harbour.

Once aboard the vessel, Yiannis was particularly impressed. He asked Nikos about the mechanics and the difficulty of sailing it in rough waters. His host was happy to tell him all about the yacht, because this was his pride and joy.

Once the ladies were seated, Yiannis helped Nikos to raise the anchor and they began their sail across to Nisyros. Although he would never admit to it, Yiannis could see that sailing the boat was now a much more difficult task for Nikos than it was before the accident, when he was able bodied. He admired the young man's bravery and applauded his determination to continue with life as normal.

Laura had been to Nisyros with Nikos before, but her mother had only been on the tourist boats with members of the family. Today Jenny felt special. She felt as though every eye was on her as she left the harbour on this very expensive yacht. She smiled inwardly as she thought about the opulent and lavish lifestyle her daughter was about to marry into and embark upon.

Arriving on Nisyros they decided not to visit the volcano today, as each of them had already been there and trekked down into the crater, which was somewhat smelly. Even though it had last erupted some one hundred and fifty thousand years ago, the heat there was still intense. Without anyone saying it, they also all knew that the trek would be impossible for Nikos, although they also knew he would have attempted it rather than show defeat.

The volcano was high on the list for tourists to visit, as parts of the 'James Bond' movie, 'Moonraker' had been filmed there.

The four went instead to the Nisyros capital, Mandraki, with its narrow streets and little shops. They found a suitable taverna that overlooked the sea and settled to relax. The view from there was clear and they could see the bay of Kamari across the water.

Both men sat and talked, whilst the women visited the shops. Laura particularly liked to shop here on this island as there was a law that prevented the shop holders from harassing people to go into their shops, and any hard sell tactics were also against the law. For these reasons, you could browse with comfort. They picked up some little gifts for the children and some fancies for the guests at the wedding breakfast. Shopping completed, they re-joined the men and went for ice cream, which was delicious.

All in all it had been a truly relaxing and enjoyable day, after which they returned to the task of wedding planning with renewed energy.

They'd decided to hold the wedding ceremony and reception in the cove where they had first gone after they met. They had arranged for a large marquee to be delivered and erected, complete with catering equipment, tables and chairs, along with a dance floor. A gazebo was to be erected on the sand, with sufficient chairs for all the guests to sit under. An arch was constructed, under which the couple would stand for the ceremony.

Boats were chartered to bring all the staff and guests to the cove, and flowers had been ordered to decorate the gazebo and arch, with lighting for the inside of the marquee.

Laura and Nikos had been to see the priest from the village and he was happy to conduct the ceremony for the man whom he'd baptised all those years ago. In sadder times, the same priest had comforted Nikos at his mum and dad's funeral.

With everything arranged it was now in the lap of the gods. They prayed for a day with good weather, not too hot, not too windy, but definitely with no rain. Unfortunately, no amount of money could arrange that feature.

With the wedding now getting closer by the day, Laura was looking forward to seeing her family and meeting the friends of Nikos, along with his work colleagues and acquaintances.

Her wedding dress hung in the spare bedroom along with the bridesmaids' attire. Her own special tiara, with the three perfectly aligned stars, sat waiting for her on the dressing table.

She thought about what had brought her to this point, the choices she'd made, rightly or wrongly that had affected her, and those experiences completely out of her control which had hurt her so deeply. Most of all she thought about the happiness she now felt.

She would marry Nikos, the man she loved so much and who she was sure loved her back also, although little doubts kicked in now and then about the dream Nikos had about having children, a dream which she was sure she could never make come true.

As she stood there on the front balcony she still marvelled at the beautiful view before her, the harbour with its many boats, the bay with many moored yachts offshore, the lovely long sweep of the bay itself, with its hotels and bars and restaurants. She looked to the little island of Kastri, a place so special to so many people who'd been married there and to the island of Nisyros on the horizon. Finally she looked at, and was mesmerised by the coastline of Turkey. This island of Kos was truly a beautiful place to live, and she felt blessed to be making Kefalos her home.

A hen party seemed a bit of a strange thought to Laura, but Jeanie had insisted she had one. During her time here on the island, Laura had made friends with the bikers' wives and girlfriends, so they were invited to join her at the Hen Party. Mum declined the invitation by saying she felt too old to go gallivanting.

The party decided to go to a restaurant that had a display of Greek dancing, where diners where encouraged to join in with the fun. There was also more modern music for the younger generation in attendance, played later in the evening when alcohol fuelled the dancing.

They arranged for a minibus to take them and collect them later from the restaurant, so everyone could enjoy themselves without needing to drive, or ride home. They enjoyed a lovely meal, complete with too much wine and free shots provided by the owner.

They watched the Greek dancing and joined in, especially when the band played, 'Zorbas-Dance,' which always got the tourists up from their seats! It was a good night and everyone enjoyed it. Although she'd not really wanted a Hen Night, Laura was happy she'd agreed to it.

Now with just a few more days remaining as a single woman, she lay on the bed pondering about the wedding. She didn't doubt she loved Nikos, but just hoped he would be happy with her. She drifted off to sleep with her future husband filling her dreams.

A Few days before the wedding, the first of the guests from England arrived. It was Suzie, her husband and their two daughters. It was arranged for them to stay at Laura's house, the house she would be leaving shortly to begin her married life with Nikos.

Laura drove to the airport to collect them and there were plenty of hugs and lots of tears when they finally came out of the arrivals lounge. It was fabulous for Laura to see her sister and to see how much her children had grown since she'd left

England. They climbed into the car and Laura piled everything into the boot.

"Nice car, Laura," Suzie observed.

"It's one of the cars Nikos owns," Laura pointed out.

"One of them," Suzie remarked. "Nikos has so many, I suppose." It was said, and meant as a joke, and Laura accepted it as such. Seat belts were fastened and they began their journey from the airport to the village of Kefalos.

Suzie had been to Kos before, for her mother's wedding to Yiannis. She'd also been for a short break before having the children, and like the rest of the family, she'd also fallen in love with Kefalos. She remembered every bend in the road, the signs to the various beaches, Sunny, Exotic, Marcus, Lagarda, Volcania and the ever famous, Paradise beach, followed by the signpost on the opposite side of the road for Kocholari, this being the last signpost before the sweeping bend that gave the visitors their first glimpse of the bay of Kamari with the little island of Kastri.

The children looked eagerly out of the car windows anticipating the fun they would have in the crystal clear, but icy cold waters of the bay.

Laura showed them to their rooms and Suzie admired the change in decor which Laura had made since she'd taken over the house from her mother.

Laura's brother, James and his wife, Caitlin would arrive tomorrow. They'd stopped here before when they'd visited their mother shortly after she'd moved here. They'd been to Kefalos a few times, when they could manage to take time off together from their busy jobs at the hospital. Laura's mother, Jenny, would be picking them up from the airport as they were staying with her and Yiannis.

Laura knew how happy her mother would be to see her only son and his wife. She also smiled to herself when she thought that everything seemed to be coming together quite beautifully, and this made her very, very happy.

CHAPTER 14
THE BIG DAY ARRIVES

Laura watched whilst the little bridesmaids had their hair plaited and tiny white Flowers were fastened on the braid. She thought they looked so cute. She felt a pang of regret, as she would love to have a child and so would Nikos, but it wasn't meant to be.

Whilst the girls held their posies whilst photographs were taken, Suzie, having had her hair finished came over to speak to Laura.

"Well Laura, this is your big day so enjoy it. Remember that for every second of the day, you are a Princess. For one day, everyone will be watching you. You are a celebrity now. I can see the headlines in the newspaper tomorrow – 'Girl Marries Millionaire' – Enjoy it, Laura."

"Don't say that," Laura snapped. "To me he's just Nikos, and everything else doesn't matter." Suzie raised her eyebrows.

"Well, whatever you think you have one hell of a life in front of you," Suzie stated. "Good luck sweetheart. See you at the ceremony."

Suzie left with the two girls, leaving her mother, Jenny, and her friend, Jeanie behind. Jeanie came across to talk with her.

"Good luck my friend. I hope we can still be friends now that you are the boss's wife and moving up in the world." She winked at Laura to confirm she was joking.

When Laura's hair was finished and her tiny tiara fixed in place, Mum helped her daughter put on the dress. As she did so, Jenny became a little emotional.

"Stop it Mum," Laura pleaded.

"I was just thinking how proud your dad would have been seeing his little baby marry today," Jenny gushed.

"I wish he'd been here," Laura said.

"Me too," said her mum. Laura looked at Jenny and looked confused. "Oh no," Jenny protested. "I love Yiannis with all my heart, honestly I do. He is a wonderful man, but I would have loved to see your dad's face today. John would have been so proud to walk you down the aisle."

"I know Mum," Laura said. "Anyway, we all love Yiannis and I for one will be proud to have him by my side today." Hearing her daughter say this made Jenny very happy.

"Right," Jenny said, "I'm going now. See you on the other side. Darling, you look wonderful. I will tell Yiannis you will be there soon."

Now Laura was alone again but she was no longer lonely as she'd once been. Mum lived nearby and the rest of her family were only four hours away. And now she was marrying Nikos, she would never be lonely again. Thinking about her future husband made her feel the butterflies dancing in her stomach.

Ready now, she walked into the lounge. Yiannis stood and offered his arm. "Shall we go?" he beamed. Laura answered with a nervous smile. "You'll be fine," Yiannis assured her.

"Yiannis," she said. "You may not be my real father, but I am honoured to have you giving me away today. Thank you."

He kissed her affectionately on the cheek. "Come on," he said. "We have a show to put on."

They arrived at the harbour and as she manoeuvred herself out of the car she was received with a cheer from a little crowd of tourists and well-wishers, who'd heard about this celebrity wedding. She caught sight of the yacht, her taxi to the wedding ceremony and could see flowers everywhere. Yiannis and Laura climbed on board.

"Ready?" asked the skipper.

"Ready," Yiannis answered. They sailed out of the harbour and round the headland, where she knew a certain someone very special was waiting for her.

Many people had been busy from early that morning. Chairs and tables, arches, floral tributes, table decorations, a large gazebo and a very large marquee had all been brought to the cove. A little jetty had been constructed so that guests could get easily from the boats to the shore. A wide length of carpet ran from the shoreline to the gazebo which housed covered chairs set out in long rows, and ropes with flowers were placed the entire length of the walk up to the arch. Everyone was busy, ensuring that everything was perfect, and this would be a wedding to remember.

Nikos was a well-loved member of the Kefalos community and the villagers loved the fact that although he was so rich, he still wanted to live in his birthplace with them. He was proud to be from Kefalos and had given back to the community in many ways over the years, funding various community projects. Now the locals wanted to say 'thank you' by making this day very special for him and his lovely wife to be. No detail was overlooked and it seemed that everyone and everything was now ready.

As the sun lost some of its ferocity, it was time for the guests to arrive. It seemed the entire village had finished work early to be there.

One after the other, boats began to cruise into the cove bringing guests from near and far. There were even some celebrities who the youngsters were quick to point out, although Laura had no clue as to who they were.

Nikos, along with Jeanie's husband, Yiannis, arrived on the black yacht. Dressed in matching short sleeved white linen shirts and black trousers, they walked together up the carpet to the seats nearest the arch. Nikos smiled at everyone and acknowledged their presence. On the outside he looked completely composed, but inside, his stomach was performing somersaults!

All the guests had now arrived and were seated in readiness for the ceremony. Now there was only Laura and Yiannis to arrive, and everyone waited in excitement to see the bride.

A white yacht sailed round the coastline. It seemed that every inch of it was covered in Flowers. Laura sat on a chair on the deck with her mother's husband, Yiannis, who was so proud to be stepping in for her father to give her away. The yacht moored next to the jetty and Yiannis helped Laura disembark. She looked radiant, as all brides are meant to look. As her feet touched the carpet the music began to play, but not the traditional wedding march, because that had seemed inappropriate here. As Nikos turned to watch his bride approach the wedding arch, he felt such love for Laura.

The ceremony was conducted in both Greek and English, with Laura and Nikos both choosing to add their own vows to each other, as well as the traditional marriage ceremony.

At the completion of the service, the priest placed a headdress on each of their heads and they were joined together with a long ribbon. He then crossed his hand and switched the headdress from one to the other. Now joined together, the happy couple took their first steps as man and wife. This was a walk Nikos had feared he would never be able to make, only a few months ago.

There were tears and screams of joy as the couple kissed in front of the congregation. They then walked hand in hand to the marquee, where they took their place at the top table. As guests began to enter behind them champagne was given to all, with fizzy drinks handed to the younger members.

After all the courses had been served, with the food being consumed and plates removed it was time for speeches. When they were over, it was now time for the traditional father and daughter dance. Laura's brother James stood to announce it.

"I have the great pleasure of taking on this role that, had he been here, my father would have taken with pride. The song we have picked would have been Dad's choice. So come on my beautiful baby sister - let's dance."

The song 'I Loved You First' was played for them, and there was not a dry eye in the house as Laura and her brother glided beautifully across the floor together. When the song was finished, James called for Nikos to join them on the dance floor.

"She's all yours now Nikos," James offered, then added, "Please take care of her."

"Always," Nikos replied. "Don't worry about that."

They slowly moved around the dance floor, Nikos had practised so hard to be perfect for this most important dance. After the first dance between husband and wife, came the traditional Greek dancing. Everyone stood and joined in with shouts of 'OPA.'

All too soon it was over, the end of a truly fabulous day. Nikos led Laura to the white yacht, where they climbed on board and waved to their guests until completely out of sight. The limousine took them from the harbour to the villa, where Nikos opened the door and skilfully picked up Laura.

"Nikos, be careful," she pleaded, knowing he was struggling a little to lift her. Once over the threshold, he quickly put her down.

"I had to do that, it's a tradition," he said smiling. "And now I want to complete another tradition." Nikos held out his hand. "Shall we adjourn to the bedroom?"

"I think it would be rude not to," Laura laughed.

"Come my wife, let's consummate this marriage," Nikos smiled.

"Gladly my husband," Laura replied. "Let us consummate this marrage all night long!"

CHAPTER 15
LOSS

Married life agreed with them both. Despite the new found wealth she found herself in, Laura took a part time job which she loved as it gave her a sense of independence, as well as her own money.

Nikos now only went to the office when it was absolutely necessary, doing much of his work online from his home office, so that he and Laura could have the opportunity to spend a lot more time together.

They began each day by taking breakfast together under the shade of the pergola, with lunch in the garden sheltered from the wind. After lunch they would go for a siesta, usually beginning with frenzied love making and then a much deserved and well earned restful nap. They ate late in the evening, sitting outside by the pool and enjoying the moonlight. They always watched the moon mirrored over the sea far below. They were happy and content.

Before the accident, Nikos had always been the sporty type. He loved to windsurf, sail and water ski. Since the accident he'd worked endlessly to perfect his walking skills, although he knew he would always walk with a slight limp. However, he also knew that even though his new lifestyle was vastly different from his old one, the alternative would have been to have died in the accident, so any lifestyle now was better than that!

He had taught Laura how to sail the yacht and they went out on the ocean as often as possible. She was so proud of him for accepting what life had thrown at him. He worked so hard at whatever task he had to master, always coming out triumphant.

He worked really hard every day in the home gymnasium, the result being that his once weakened body was now starting to tone up nicely into an athletic, muscular one again.

Laura really enjoyed living at the Villa. It still felt a little like she was visiting a luxury hotel, but she soon began to add her own personality by adding lamps and soft furnishings to add a little feminine touch to what had been a very masculine 'bachelor pad.' She also loved to work in the garden with Costas. She designed areas of the garden and Costas supplied the muscle that brought it to reality.

As the season came to a close, the resort fell quiet. Many who had worked in the resort returned to their homes in the village, or some left to spend winter in Athens, so the pace of life slowed. Despite this, it was a much needed resting time for the people of Kefalos.

Laura still loved to walk and many early mornings she would travel down the road to the now deserted beach. Sometimes she swam then returned to the house to wake her sleeping husband.

One such morning when she was alone she'd walked along the edge of the sea, dipping her toes in the water occasionally and was mesmerised by the waves this morning as they crashed onto the sand.

She was scrambling over the rocks at the far end of the beach when her foot slipped and she landed on top of the rock with a bang. It shocked her and it knocked the breath out of her, but she wasn't really hurt. She now felt stupid to have come this far alone, with nobody actually knowing where she had gone. If she'd really hurt herself it would have taken a long time to find her, especially if no one was looking!

She brushed the sand and seaweed from her clothes and began the long walk back to the car. By the time she arrived home, Nikos was sitting on the veranda sipping his coffee. She told him what had happened and he laughed at her.

"You should be more careful, darling," he said. "You are not a mountain goat to go climbing over the rocks."

Although she wasn't expecting it, the next day she started her period. She thought nothing of it when it ended the next day. 'Nature can be perverse,' she told herself, 'a period lasting only twenty-four hours!'

Life carried on as normal. As newlyweds they made love frequently and savoured their time together. One day she felt a little dizzy and queasy, but it quickly passed so she forgot about it. However, a couple of days after the twenty-four hour period, she got up as usual went to the bathroom to shower, but promptly vomited. Nikos heard her being sick.

"What's the matter, Laura?" he shouted to her, concerned.

"I think it might have been last night's prawns," she replied, brushing it off.

"Are you saying my cooking did not agree with you?" he joked, but when it happened again the following day, Nikos insisted she see the doctor.

The next day at the surgery the doctor asked a few general questions, but then asked more seriously, "Is it possible you might be pregnant?"

"No," Laura answered. "That's impossible because I cannot have children."

"And why might that be?" the doctor questioned.

"Before meeting Nikos I was in a previous relationship with a man called Martin," Laura explained to the doctor. "We tried for a family for a long time, but it just didn't happen."

"Did you or your husband, have tests to see if you could conceive or not?" the doctor questioned.

"No," Laura answered with honesty, although without telling the medical man that she and Martin were never married. "Martin always said it was stupid, as there was nothing wrong with him. He always blamed me."

"It seems like this man was in denial, Laura," the doctor stated. "If it's okay with you, I would like to do a few tests on you. Would that be a good idea?"

"Sounds okay to me," Laura replied.

She was given a small container and sent to the bathroom to provide a urine sample. Whilst supplying the sample, she noticed a small amount of blood in her pee and returned to tell the doctor.

"I think I may have started my period," she revealed.

"Is it due?" he questioned.

"Well I must admit, I'm confused," she admitted.

"And why is that?" the doctor asked.

Laura told the doctor about what had happened a few days earlier when she thought she was starting a period, but it had stopped the next day.

"Don't worry," the doctor said, trying to be as calm as possible. "We will run a few tests and see just what's going on with you." After drawing a blood sample he asked, "Can you come back tomorrow?" Laura agreed.

That night Laura woke up with severe stomach pain, which was obviously not good! Nikos phoned the Hospital and the doctor told them to come to the medical centre immediately. By the time they arrived, Laura was in excruciating pain and was bleeding profusely. This was no normal period!

After the doctor conducted a full examination, he spoke softly to Laura "I'm sorry to tell you, but I think you are suffering a miscarriage. I would like to admit you immediately."

Laura was confused. "It can't be that," she said.

"Well let's see shall we?" the doctor suggested.

A little later Laura was whisked off to the theatre, where it was confirmed that she had indeed suffered a miscarriage. Nikos sat holding her hand as she wept; crying because she felt it was her fault as the fall on the rocks had probably caused it.

She felt useless again remembering the dream Nikos had told her about having a family. As Nikos looked worryingly at her, she looked grey. In her mind she just kept thinking of what might have been.

"I estimate that you were around two months pregnant when you miscarried," the doctor explained when she was returned to her room. "However there is no permanent damage and no reason why you cannot get pregnant again in the future, but please take some time to recuperate."

Upon hearing this sad but also wonderful news, Laura looked at Nikos to see he was now very emotional. "Laura, my dream about children is still a possibility," was all he could say before putting his head in his hands and sobbing like a baby.

"I'll leave you for a little while but then, Nikos, I suggest you allow your wife to get some rest," the doctor instructed.

"Thank you doctor," Nikos said through the tears, but at least they were now happy tears of joy.

A few days later, Laura left the medical centre and returned home. It was if a fire within her had been put out. Her eyes had lost their sparkle, she was sullen and quiet and she didn't want to leave the house. Nikos tried to comfort her but she would have none of it, making him feel useless. She just kept pushing him away more and more.

"You should never have married me" she said. "I told you I couldn't have children but you wouldn't listen, and now look at us. I have ruined everything!" She was inconsolable."

Days passed and they hardly spoke. Laura finally suggested she should go and spend some time at her own house. Nikos in desperation agreed that a mini separation might help, so she packed few things and left him standing on the front porch of the villa.

Laura told her mother she was going back to the house. Jenny was concerned for her daughter and offered to come round and take care of her, but Laura said she wanted to spend some time on her own to deal with all that had happened. Although her mother didn't think this was the best course of action, she did as she was asked and stayed away. She did, however, phone everyday without fail. Sometimes

Laura answered, but more often she did not. When she did answer, the conversations were short.

"I'm okay, I just want to be left alone," Laura kept saying. Jenny phoned Nikos and he told her that he was getting the same reaction.

Laura was slipping back further each day and returning to the wreck she once was when she'd first arrived in Kefalos. She felt useless, that she was no good at anything! She felt like she wasn't a good wife to Nikos. It must be her fault, as it was her fault her first relationship with Martin had ended.

She wasn't enough for Martin, so he was entitled to find someone else. It must have been her fault that Martin found comfort in the bed of another – her best friend!

Martin had wanted a family, just as Nikos did now, but she couldn't give either of them the children they so desired. Laura felt totally useless, a waste of space! She thought about Nikos and how he had so many female companions. Perhaps one of them could give him the child he wanted.

The depression was so deep now that she stopped eating properly, with her personal hygiene becoming almost non-existent! Her hair was greasy and matted and her clothes needed washing, making her smell a little stinky!

She knew she needed to take better care of herself, but there was no point. There was no one to see her and she didn't want to see anyone else. She felt sorry and guilty about the fact that she'd agreed to marry Nikos when she knew the situation regarding her failing to fall pregnant. Even more worryingly, she wondered who would really miss her if she wasn't there. She was so unhappy and felt a complete failure at everything.

She sat on the couch with her legs tucked underneath her and draped an old cardigan around her for comfort as she rocked back and forth on the seat. Was she beginning to lose her mind? Even when Nikos phoned and said he would take her out, she declined his offer. She had lost all interest in life!

Weeks passed and Nikos could not stand it any longer. He drove to Laura's house and hammered on the door. After several minutes, she finally answered. He looked at her and was shocked at her appearance. She was a mess, unwashed and wearing scruffy clothes! She also looked pale and skinny. He guessed she hadn't eaten properly for some time.

"Can I come in?" Nikos questioned.

"No," she told him defiantly. "I want to be on my own. It's better all round that way. Go, Nikos, and get on with your own life. I'm okay."

Nikos ignored Laura and gently pushed past her and into the house. Just like the girl he loved, the interior of the house was also a mess! Clothes were piled high in front of the washing machine, uneaten food was left on the table and unwashed cups and plates had been thrown in the sink.

Oh, Laura, what has happened to you?" he sighed. She couldn't look at him.

He walked across to her, picked her up and carried her to the bathroom where he put her down near the shower and gently undressed her. She put up no resistance as he placed her under the showerhead. He watched as she slowly lathered herself in soap and bubbles, rinsed off and stepped out of the shower.

Lovingly Nikos wrapped a large towel around her and led her to the bedroom. She sat on the bed like a frightened child whilst he softly patted her body until she was dry. All the time he was doing this she was looking at him with her once beautiful eyes, which now seemed to be sunken into her head where she'd lost so much weight. He had to admit, she looked dreadful.

Laura eventually looked directly at Nikos and finally spoke. "I'm so sorry, Nikos, I didn't mean to do it. I slipped but didn't know. I'm so sorry."

"Laura, it's not your fault," he said, hoping to make her feel better. "I'm sure we can get through this together." But Laura wasn't sure she could get through it. She would always have the feeling that she'd taken his dream away again.

He put his arms around her but she felt very frail as she clung to him. He held her as if she were a fragile, porcelain China doll, who might break should he hold her too tightly. His hand caressed her neck and shoulders as she stood naked before him.

Nikos looked at the bed. Laura looked at the bed and then back at him. She slid under the blanket and Nikos began to undress. Laura watched his every move, remembering how much she loved, and missed his body. As he climbed in beside her she rested her head on his chest. Ever so slowly, he stroked her frail body then leaned over and kissed her lips, cheeks and her throat.

"Oh Nikos," she softly moaned in the ecstasy of the moment. He kissed her breast and she began to respond. They made beautiful, but gentle love. This was what they both needed, a release on so many levels.

When the lovemaking was finished, Laura fell into a deep sleep and Nikos held her in his arms whilst she slept. He hoped and prayed for this to be a fresh start and she could begin to heal.

"Tomorrow, I will take you home where you belong," he whispered to her as she slept. He stayed the night just holding her, the woman he loved more than life itself.

CHAPTER 16
A FRESH START

Slowly they rekindled their relationship. Every day Laura thought of the miscarriage she'd suffered and grieved, but day by day she was becoming stronger and she learnt to love Nikos all over again. She still felt the guilt but knew she would get over it, although she knew it would be a slow process.

Jeanie called to see her. She knew Laura had been very depressed and wanted to help her friend in any way she could. Laura had refused to talk about what had happened but Jeanie wanted her to do so, as it was part of the healing process.

"I'd rather not," Laura protested.

"But you should talk about it sweetheart, it will help. I promise you," Jeanie told her beautiful friend. "I know how you feel"

"How could you possibly know how I feel?" Laura claimed angrily. "You haven't been through it."

"I do know, because it HAS happened to me," Jeanie admitted. "It has happened to me three times!"

"What? – When? – How....?" Laura queried, looking baffled.

"Did you not think it was strange that a woman married to a Greek did not have any children, even though they've been married for a few years?

"I'm sorry, I didn't know," Laura said apologetically.

"Having children is so important to Greeks, and God only knows we have tried," Jeanie confessed. "This is one of the reasons why my mother-in-law doesn't like me. She thinks her son should never have married me. She believes that if he'd married a Greek woman instead of a foreigner, he would have lots of children running around now, enough to fill their home. Instead, he chose me and we have no children. So Laura, I do know how exactly you feel."

"Jeanie, I am so sorry," Laura stated. "So what happened?"

"The first pregnancy was over almost as quickly as it had started. In fact it was over so quickly that we hadn't time to tell anyone," Jeanie claimed. "The second time I was half expecting it to happen again, but when it did, I was just as mortified. This time Yiannis's mother did know about the pregnancy and she was the first to criticise me when I lost the baby. When I got pregnant the third time, she handed out old wives tales about how to ensure I carried it to full term. This time it was more devastating than the previous two.

I was further into my pregnancy and had supposedly passed the dangerous three months. This time it felt more real and we thought this time it would be okay. We even had a name for the baby. When we lost her, I thought it was the end for Yiannis and me, but this time we had guidance and support from a charity that helps women who suffer miscarriages. I will give you the details, Laura, you should speak to them. They are fantastic."

Jeanie heaved a huge sigh of relief at getting this off her chest. Laura felt terrible at how selfish she'd been, how cruel she'd been not to have considered others. She apologised profusely to her friend and they hugged tightly and for what seemed like forever.

"Will you speak to the lady from the charity," Jeanie asked.

Laura thought long and hard before she answered. Could this help her? Maybe it could should she take a chance of seeing the counsellor. It wouldn't bring back her baby but it might help her move on.

"Okay, I will go," she said to Jeanie.

Laura went to see the counsellor from the miscarriage charity. She learned that miscarriage was far more common than she'd thought. The counsellor explained to Laura that they found people didn't want to talk about it and kept it secret. Some never got over the experience and some women even take their own lives.

As Laura listened, she was reliving her own feelings and related them to everything the counsellor was saying. It had been heart breaking, yet Jeanie had had this experience three times. How could she ever get over that?

Laura attended several sessions. Nikos joined her on a couple of occasions and it seemed to help him too.

"So, how's it going with the counsellor?" Jeanie asked when she saw Laura next.

"Very well," Laura told her. "I've cried, I've been angry, I've felt regret, I have grieved, but now I've moved on a little and now have hope for the future. One day I will have a child and make Nikos's dream come true, I am sure of it."

"I am so pleased you are feeling that way now because I have something to tell you," Jeanie announced. "I was afraid to tell you before, but as you are progressing each day I feel I can tell you now. I'm about four months pregnant now, so I'm passed the danger mark of three months. I am being closely monitored, have loads of support and everything is going well."

"That's amazing news, Jeanie," Laura said with genuine happiness. "I am so pleased for you and Yiannis."

"Thank you, Laura. They say that if you have a baby after you have suffered a miscarriage it's called a Rainbow Baby. I am praying that this will be our rainbow baby. I pray that you will soon also have a Rainbow Baby," Jeanie remarked, and Laura hugged her again.

"I am so delighted for you, Jeanie. I will be here to support you every inch of the way, just as you have supported me" Laura stated.

"Let's hope that one day we can support each other," was Jeanie's parting gift.

CHAPTER 17
INCREDIBLE NEWS

"Laura, did you forget about your appointment yesterday?" It was her doctor phoning from the clinic.

"Oh my, I am so sorry," Laura replied. "Yes, I totally forgot."

"Don't worry. Can you come today?" he questioned. "I have your results here, but do not wish to tell you over the phone."

"Can you take me to the clinic, Nikos?" Laura questioned her husband.

"Of course," he replied.

"We'll be there soon," Laura told the medical man.

While Laura went inside the medical centre, Nikos stayed in the car. Seeing her alone made the doctor look a little puzzled.

"Is your husband not with you" he questioned.

"He's waiting outside in the car," Laura said.

"I think we should have a word with him also, shouldn't we?" the doctor suggested.

"Is it bad news? Is something wrong?" Laura asked, feeling nervous now.

"Let's wait for Nikos," the doctor suggested.

Nikos was sent for and came in and sat down next to Laura, immediately holding her hand. He also now had a concerned look on his face as he looked directly towards the doctor.

"I have some news for you both," the doctor began. "Laura, I am pleased to tell you that you are pregnant. Nikos, you are going to be a father."

Nikos jumped out of his chair as quickly as his leg would allow and punched the air. His happiness at the news was incredible. He clapped his hands together, kissed Laura and shook the doctor by the hand.

"We did it!" he cried. "My dream – sorry - our dream is happening for real!"

Laura was speechless. Did she dare believe what she was hearing? She asked the doctor for confirmation. "Isn't it too early to tell if I'm pregnant or not? Could the same thing happen again – a miscarriage? I haven't missed a period that I know of."

"The shock of the miscarriage could have upset your cycle, Laura. Let's see shall we," the doctor said, speaking softly to try to reassure her and Nikos. "I will arrange a scan in a couple of weeks and see what that tells us. In the meantime take care, but celebrate the news.

When Jeanie went into Labour, Laura was there to support her. Yiannis was in America dealing with the final details of the sale of a super yacht, so Laura went to hospital with Jeanie and held her hands throughout her Labour.

Jeanie's baby daughter was delivered safely, followed by many tears of joy for the two women. Once it was confirmed by the doctor that everything was okay, Laura sat down next to the bed watching Jeanie feed her baby named, Poppy. She was very moved by the whole emotional experience.

Knowing that Jeanie had suffered three miscarriages before yet she was here with a baby in her arms filled Laura with hope for her own impending motherhood.

"Jeanie, I have something to tell you," Laura said, grabbing her friend's attention. "Remember you told me that you prayed for me to also have a 'Rainbow' Baby?"

"Yes," Jeanie replied with curiosity.

"Well, although it's still a bit of a secret, and very early days, I found out this week that I'm pregnant," Laura gushed. "I am expecting a baby in the spring."

"I am so very pleased for you, sweetheart," Jeanie told her friend with a beaming smile. "I hope everything works out for you, as it did for me. And just think, one day, Poppy and your baby can be playmates." Both the women happily laughed at this thought.

Laura's pregnancy progressed. She spoke to the counsellor from the charity and he was thrilled for her, but still offered support to Laura and Nikos throughout the pregnancy, "Just in case anything goes wrong."

She read all the literature available about pregnancy and early childcare and Nikos did the same. He was very supportive all through her pregnancy and they chatted about what stage the baby's development was at. When she first felt the baby kick, it was the confirmation Laura needed for her to realise there was a tiny human growing inside her. It was a period of grieving for what might have been, and a period of hope and expectation for what was to come.

Laura was now blooming, an absolute picture of health. As the weeks passed, she became more and more confident that this time she would carry the baby full term. Frequent checks were made and everything was perfectly normal. The baby was growing well. The heartbeat was strong, and movement of the baby was felt regularly. The kicks soon became cause for laughter for the expectant mum and dad.

It was now approaching the expected date for the baby to arrive. Laura had been preparing for the arrival by buying bits and pieces over the past month or so. Nikos and she had planned the nursery together, buying furniture, bedding, and coordinating curtains. A rocking chair was installed under the window for Laura to use when nursing the baby, and thanks to Nikos's enthusiasm, large soft toys filled the shelves. There was an intercom wired so that every sound could be heard in the house, should the baby start to cry. This was connected to a light in the bedroom which would flash in the night, just in case they slept through the cries.

The best buggy money could buy, with all its various attachments sat in another building by the swimming pool, as Laura had been told it was bad luck to have the pram at the house before the baby arrived. Laura was leaving nothing to chance!

With everything ready, the anxious expectant parents waited for the arrival of their first child.

Laura had decided not to go to Rhodes or Athens to have their baby delivered, she would instead go to the medical centre and put her safety in the hands of the doctor who'd previously looked after her. He would be the man to deliver their baby.

As the time drew ever closer, Laura wobbled round the garden carrying an old-fashioned fan to cool her, as she was really suffering with the heat. Her feet and legs were swollen and it had become uncomfortable to sit for long periods. She still couldn't believe it was happening now, when all that time with Martin, she'd tried for a baby and it hadn't happened. She now thought 'thank God it didn't happen then,' as she would probably now be locked in a loveless marriage.

Now feeling as big as a house, Laura had been told that if the baby didn't make an appearance within the next two days, she would have to go into hospital to be induced. This was something she didn't like the sound of!

A little walk down the Hill to the beach wouldn't do any harm, she thought, as she put on some comfy shoes and walked out of the front door and down the driveway. Costas was in the garden working on the flower beds. He waved to her and she shouted to him, "If Nikos wakes up, please tell him I went for a little walk down to the beach."

It was definitely more difficult to walk any great distance with this oversized football in front of her, and it took a lot of effort to walk down the steep road to the harbour but finally she reached her intended destination. As she sat on the wall and looked at the boats, her breathing finally returned to normal.

The tourist trip boats were moored in the harbour, whilst as ever at this time in the morning the fishermen were

147

readying their boats for today's catch. It all seemed so calm and tranquil this morning.

Laura thought about all the times she'd been told by many different people that Kos heals the body and the soul, and they were correct. She'd come here as a broken woman but had now found happiness beyond her wildest dreams.

She felt a strong kick, as if the baby were tuning into her thoughts. "Yes, little one," she said out loud, "a wonderful life awaits you when you are ready to meet us."

She stood up from the bench and began the walk up the hill, but if walking down was difficult, the return journey was really hard work but she persevered. Her body began to ache and her legs felt so heavy, as each step became harder. The pressure on her pelvis was becoming more and more unbearable, so she stopped by the little church to catch her breath. Not being one for praying, she still however muttered under her breath, "Lord help me get home safely."

Somebody 'up there' must have been listening, for as she started to walk again, after only walking a little further a black four by four rounded the bend and stopped right next to her. It was Nikos.

"Laura, are you okay?" he questioned. "I was sleeping and thought I heard you calling me. Costas said you'd gone for a walk, so I came to look for you."

"Oh, thank you Nikos," Laura smiled. "It was such hard work walking back up the Hill."

As she attempted to climb in the car, her body was suddenly rocked by a horrific pain. She leaned into the car until the pain passed.

"Nikos I think the baby is coming," she announced.

"What, now?" Nikos shouted in panic.

"Let's get my bag from the villa and go straight to the medical centre," Laura almost pleaded.

Nikos drove quickly to the house and picked up the bag which Laura had left ready for this moment. It contained her clothes and cosmetics, along with an outfit for the baby.

When he emerged from the house, Nikos could see Laura with her head down as she was just getting over another contraction.

He drove quickly, but as carefully as possible to the medical centre, having phoned them in advance to let them know they were on their way. Upon arrival, Laura was ushered directly into the delivery room. The doctor, who had now become a firm friend was there to greet them.

Laura continued to have sporadic contractions all through the day and was connected to a foetal monitor, which was closely scrutinised by the attending nurse.

The sky was darkening as the evening approached, when the doctor came and praised Laura for her stamina. He reviewed the printout on the monitor.

"Laura, if the baby's heart rate doesn't stop fluctuating, we may have to consider giving you some help," he announced.

Laura was not sure what he meant by that, so questioned, "What do you mean?"

"I'll give you another twenty minutes, but then we will review the situation," he replied, but she was still none the wiser.

When the doctor was gone, Nikos could see the fear in Laura's eyes. He leaned over and kissed her.

"Come on darling, we can do this," he said. "Our baby is coming and we will soon have an extended family." The smile on his face was precious and made Laura feel blessed.

She suddenly experienced a new, different sensation, which now made her want to push. Nikos rang the call bell and the doctor came.

"It seems I scared the little one into getting a move on," he joked. "Now it's time for the hard work, Laura. That's why they call it labour. Are you ready to help your baby come into the world?" Laura nodded as she squeezed Nikos's hand. Each time she had another contraction the squeeze became firmer, until almost becoming unbearable for the expectant Daddy!

At nine o'clock in the evening their baby was finally born. They had a healthy baby boy – a son – an heir. He was placed in Laura's arms and all the tiredness and pain of the previous few hours were all forgotten.

When Laura handed him to Nikos, he was overcome with emotion. He was so proud and his smile said it all. He cradled his son gently in his arms and walked to the window, where he opened the blind to a night sky full of stars. Three very bright stars in a line stood out in the sky.

"Look little one, this is where you live," he declared. "This is where you are going to have such great adventures and a wonderful life." With a smile on his face so wide that it almost hurt, he kissed the baby on the head.

Laura and Nikos were dedicated and caring parents to their son, whom they named, Dimitris after Nikos's father. When they first took the baby home they were so anxious that they were doing the right things. Just the same as any other parents, they frequently checked to make sure he was breathing when in his cot at night, and were constantly reading books on childcare.

As far as his development went they made sure he had the right stimulation, with plenty of colourful toys and lots of playful interaction. The child wanted for nothing. He was given his parents' love and attention all day every day.

They were so happy and proud of their little boy and when he first sat up on his own, it was a huge cause for celebration. When he crawled they were delighted, and Nikos was so proud when his first word was "Papa."

Nikos loved to take his son to the beach, where the two would make sandcastles. Sometimes he took him in the sea, and after the initial shock of the cold water, Dimitris loved it. He also loved to be on the yacht wearing his own little life jacket. He laughed when the wind gusted and blew his hair, or the waves splashed his face.

"He will make a good sailor," Nikos proudly told everyone.

He and Laura panicked one day when they sat Dimitris on the beach and his pudgy little hand grabbed some sand and immediately went to put it into his mouth. Laura tried to grab his hand to stop him, but he succeeded in putting some in. He coughed and spat it out.

"Laura, do you think he will be okay?" a concerned Nikos asked his wife.

"Nikos," Laura laughed. "It's what children do."

Now that he was crawling, nothing was out of reach and everything had to be considered a danger. He could get everywhere and was now starting to pull himself up with the furniture, standing for a little while before plonking himself back down on his bottom.

Laura blossomed in her role as a mother and the love for the two most important males in her life deepened each and every day.

Dimitris was now approaching three years of age. With Nikos and Laura both talking to him in their own native languages he was bilingual, speaking both Greek and English fluently.

Laura looked at him as he played on the sand. He was a good child and quite content to play on his own but she wished so much that he wasn't an only child, although she knew she'd been so lucky to have a child in the first place and she was thankful for that.

Sitting on the balcony each night, she would look at the night sky and wish on the stars for a second child. One night as she wished, a shooting star raced across the sky. Was this a sign? Laura sure hoped it was.

CHAPTER 18
BIRTHDAY PRESENT

It was Nikos's birthday, so family and friends had been invited to the Villa to celebrate. After they'd enjoyed a fabulous meal, Laura stood up to congratulate Nikos and bring in the cake.

"Now my darling," she began. "I had thought long and hard about what to get you for your birthday. Maybe a yacht, but you have one of those. Maybe a sports car, oh no, you have one of those too. So, just what do you get for the man who has everything?" Everyone smiled waiting on Laura's every word, as she continued.. "Well I found something, something I know you've wanted for a very long time." She handed him an envelope. He looked the envelope and then back at her with puzzled interest. "Open it and see," she said. Nikos opened the envelope and peered inside.

"What is it?" he asked, looking at Laura.

"Really, it's been made especially for you," she said.

Everyone was now waiting with baited breath to find out what the present was. Nikos looked visibly shaken as he read the contents of the envelope Laura had presented him with.

"My darling wife has made me very happy," Nikos finally announced, as he stood and looked around at his family and close friends. "Today, Laura is giving me a daughter!" he gushed, in a voice filled with emotion. Everyone cheered and shouted congratulations to them both.

Laura glanced at Nikos and he mouthed to her, 'Now I am a man who has everything.'

She'd kept her pregnancy a secret, not wanting to build up her, or Nikos's hopes before she was sure that everything was going to be okay. She'd secretly visited the doctor and he confirmed she was indeed pregnant, and told her what she should and should not do, given her past history.

Laura explained to the doctor how she wasn't going to tell Nikos the news until his birthday, and had sworn the doctor to secrecy. He gave her tablets to suppress her morning sickness and also told her how pleased he was for her. An early scan had revealed the sex of the baby and Laura was thrilled to discover she was carrying a girl.

Her plan to surprise Nikos had not been easy as she was beginning to put on weight, but she managed to hide the gain just long enough to reach his birthday. She'd kept the scan picture safely in her purse, so she could attach it to the birthday card she'd just given to him. For Nikos it was the best most special birthday present he'd ever received.

Only a few weeks later, Nikos was devastated when his grandmother, who'd brought him up, had become ill and sadly passed away. Funerals were quickly arranged in Kefalos, as per tradition.

Laura sat in the church next to Nikos. She herself was finding it sad that his grandma would never see her granddaughter. They had told her about the pregnancy and she told them that she was very happy that Dimitris would have a sister to grow up with. She was especially pleased when they told her that the baby girl would be named after her.

On the way from the funeral to the cemetery the coffin was paraded through the village, where people lined the streets to pay their respects. Eventually the body was placed in the family grave where Nikos's parents had been placed.

Many gathered afterwards to drink a toast to the wonderful woman, who having lost her son and daughter-in-law had brought up their son to be a much loved member of the community and a very successful businessman. She would be sadly missed by many, but most of all by Nikos. However, as with many times before, a new soul was about to come into the world, just as this one left it.

Laura and Nikos prepared the nursery for their expected baby. This time it was pink and pretty, with frills everywhere. Dimitris now had 'a grown up boy's' room, complete with dinosaur themed bedding and curtains. He was proud that he was to be a big brother to his sister. He frequently talked to 'the bump,' asking constantly when she would be here to play with him.

When Laura went into labour, albeit a little early, she panicked a little. She thought of her sister, Emily, who'd been born prematurely and only remained alive for a few days. She understood now how her mother and father must have felt at that time, remembering also how her own miscarriage had affected her.

She paced around the delivery room, halting from time to time to deal with the contractions which were now coming fast and furious and lasting much longer. She spoke gently to the bump as she stroked the bulge in her stomach.

"Come on little one. Mummy and Daddy are waiting to meet you. We love you so much already and your big brother cannot wait to see you."

Nikos entered the room, having rushed from a conference as soon as he'd been told that Laura had gone into labour.

"Isn't it too early?" he asked with a worried look on his face.

"A little," Laura replied, trying to reassure him even though she was also panicking inside.

The doctor came in to examine Laura and said how well she was doing. "I don't think it will be too long now. The baby will be here soon," he smiled.

Nikos looked at Laura. He loved her so deeply, for she was a remarkable woman. She had been strong for him when he needed it and she was a fabulous mother to their son, Dimitris. He squeezed her hand and kissed her forehead.

"Are you ready to be a dad again?" she asked Nikos.

"Oh yes," he proudly and excitedly replied.

154

Laura gave birth to their daughter, who as promised was named Toula, after Nikos's grandmother. They need not have worried as she was perfectly formed and breathed normally. Indeed the new parents laughed as she let out a loud cry to announce her arrival to the world!

"Welcome to the world little one," the proud parents said in unison.

Laura and Nikos took Toula home and her big brother was waiting to see his new sister. He didn't seem overly impressed at first, but finally he decided she was 'quite nice' and could stay as long as she didn't touch his toys.

The night she was born, Nikos held both his children in his arms and took them to the window to view the stars. "Tonight my dream has come true," he said. "A dream we never believed would become reality. I was always told when the stars align your wishes come true, and now they have.

I found a soul mate that loves me and wants to be with me, a soul mate who wanted to be my wife and now we have our little family, one boy and one girl – perfect."

Little Toula looked up at her daddy with big eyes as he continued. "We have been truly blessed and so will you two be. Your mother and I have so much to tell you about all the wonderful things that await you, and about this most magical place called, Kefalos, which is now your home."

Toula and Dimitris grew up in their beautiful home in the village of Kefalos. They became the happiest, healthiest, much-loved children possible. They would have lots of wonderful adventures and experiences ahead of them..........
But that's another story.

THE END

(Please turn the page to see more from Wendy)

More books by this author, Wendy Howard -

<u>LOOK</u> <u>TO</u> <u>THE</u> <u>STARS</u>

"Whenever you feel sad or alone, look to the stars and I will be there for you. I'll be with you forever." - These were the last words ever spoken to Jenny by her husband, John, as he lay on his deathbed. Moments later he died in her arms. This is her story.

Jenny is a lovely teenage girl from a wonderful family, who along with her best friend, Sue, has an enjoyment for life. This normally involves going to meet friends at 'Bob's Café,' along with meeting boys, socializing and having fun.

Both girls have a 'Sliding Doors' moment when Jenny goes on holiday with her family to Cornwall, whilst Sue goes to Mallorca. Something happens to both girls during these holidays which will change their lives forever. Life for them will never be the same again.

This is the debut novel by Wendy Howard, an author born in the North of England but who now lives in Kefalos on the beautiful Greek island of Kos, where much of this story takes place. If you love a good romance, then this could be the story for you. - Wendy's first novel, but it won't the last. This will be the first of many.

Available from your local Amazon store

Printed in Great Britain
by Amazon

29998801R00088